WALKING LEONARD
and Other Stories

Essential Prose Series 186

Guernica Editions Inc. acknowledges the support of the Canada
Council for the Arts and the Ontario Arts Council.
The Ontario Arts Council is an agency of the Government of Ontario.

We acknowledge the financial support of the Government of Canada.

WALKING LEONARD

and Other Stories

Sophie Stocking

GUERNICA EDITIONS
TORONTO • CHICAGO • BUFFALO • LANCASTER (U.K.)
2021

Copyright © 2021, Sophie Stocking and Guernica Editions Inc.
All rights reserved. The use of any part of this publication,
reproduced, transmitted in any form or by any means, electronic,
mechanical, photocopying, recording or otherwise stored
in a retrieval system, without the prior consent
of the publisher is an infringement of the copyright law.

Michael Mirolla, editor
David Moratto, interior and cover design
Guernica Editions Inc.
287 Templemead Drive, Hamilton, ON L8W 2W4
2250 Military Road, Tonawanda, N.Y. 14150-6000 U.S.A.
www.guernicaeditions.com

Distributors:
Independent Publishers Group (IPG)
600 North Pulaski Road, Chicago IL 60624
University of Toronto Press Distribution,
5201 Dufferin Street, Toronto (ON), Canada M3H 5T8
Gazelle Book Services, White Cross Mills
High Town, Lancaster LA1 4XS U.K.

First edition.
Printed in Canada.

Legal Deposit—First Quarter
Library of Congress Catalog Card Number: 2020947878
Library and Archives Canada Cataloguing in Publication
Title: Walking Leonard & other stories / Sophie Stocking.
Other titles: Walking Leonard and other stories
Names: Stocking, Sophie, 1966- author.
Series: Essential prose series ; 186.
Description: Series statement: Essential prose series ; 186
Identifiers: Canadiana (print) 2020035941X | Canadiana (ebook) 20200359428
| ISBN 9781771835848 (softcover) | ISBN 9781771835855 (EPUB)
| ISBN 9781771835862 (Kindle)
Classification: LCC PS8637.T616 W34 2021 | DDC C813/.6—dc23

*For my mother, who said
"Take notes. It will make a good story."*

Contents

Rabbit Trails	.....	1
Murdy	.....	11
Thirty-third Street	.....	27
Walking Leonard	.....	39
Intersection	.....	57
Shelterbelt	.....	71
Bobcat	.....	99
Mrs. Mobach	.....	121
Archimedes	.....	129
Acknowledgements	.....	157
About the Author	.....	159

Rabbit Trails

Somewhere in interior B.C. a girl climbs a soft-needled fir tree. The smooth bark pebbled with pockets of sap is just the kind of tree she's after. She climbs in her bare feet with a twig between her teeth, the twig stripped of bark and sharpened at one end.

Shakti settles herself a good way up, in a crook between a thick branch and the trunk. The neighbour's white jeep passes two metres beneath her feet, a rare bit of traffic on the Old Kaslo Road. They're driving to Nelson. She likes her perch, to see and not be seen, like Robin Hood. To her left lies a meadow, and along its shadowy forest edge Shakti glimpses a black bear, rooting through the huckleberry bush. Black bears are as thick as flies in the Kootenays and she pays him no particular mind.

Beneath her the plants in the ditch radiate an underlying gold. Saturated and translucent, burnt orange Turk's cap lilies, chartreuse ferns uncurling their snail shell coils, a raku-glazed beetle stalks on its wiry legs through the dust. Down the road now she hears horses. Her sister riding Friday, the dapple-grey two-year-old, and Kelly follows on a potbellied chestnut. They move on beneath her heading towards Kelly's house.

She turns back to the tree trunk. You take your sharp stick and puncture the sap bubbles under the bark, a strangely satisfying endeavour. It's a good way to spend an hour in a breathing fir tree, on a hot summer's day when you don't want to go home. By the time she's worked around a few metres of the trunk, ritually puncturing, a bank of cloud rolls over the sun and thunder grumbles low and hollow. In the waiting quiet a chainsaw comes to life and a rooster crows. In a while she'll smell the smoke of wood fires rising out of galvanized stovepipes. Women like her mother will start cooking supper.

Shakti climbs down, the soles of her feet feeling for crotches and branchless gaps, till they reach the hot talcum powder dust of the road. Hoof beats knock staccato again; she feels them through the road before she hears them. River careens around the corner, pulls back on the reins. The horse's neck arches down, feet crowding each other, and then a snort and shake of the head and a sideways look from Friday's piebald eye.

Her sister, in Levi 501's, a tight baby blue t-shirt, and her first ever pair of genuine cowboy boots, leans over and rakes her fingers through her sister's hair.

"Your hair's full of sap again. Mama's gonna take the scissors to you! You'd better get home. Daddy's *really* mad this time." River moves off, pressing the horse into a trot and on to a canter, then finally the freedom of a full gallop. Riding towards some white-bread cowgirl preferable universe. Shakti watches her go, her straight ten-year-old body in Guatemalan blouse and denim cutoffs.

She mulls over the issue of home and the best way to

approach it. This time, the third time. Which was better to delay as long as possible? Or just go humbly and beg? She decides to take the long way round, veering off the road into the shady protection of the cedars. Shakti heads east along this particular rabbit trail leading to the Skunk Cabbage Pond. Stooping, she picks a loam tasting fiddlehead and threads a Linnea flower through the buttonhole of her blouse. When she arrives, she lies on the mossy bank and watches the black water striders skate across the pond. Their six legs only dimple the surface tension. She wishes she could go like them, so lightly, or masterfully and uncaring on a horse like River.

Alisha Winter started it, the beautiful art school friend who stayed at the cabin for a week in June. She'd shown Shakti how to draw faces, the proportions, where eyes and ears sit on the skull. She had long blond hair and played "Good Night Irene" on her guitar, even better Shakti thought, than Leadbelly. Alisha smoked Marlboroughs. Didn't she know cigarettes killed people? Shakti saw them in the night, passing with a flashlight on her way to the outhouse. On the return trip she took them off the table, opened the pack and ran the silky cylinders through her fingers. Then she broke each one and threw them in the garbage. Alisha wasn't so interested in playing with little kids after that, and to Shakti's disgust she taped the cigarettes back together and smoked them, cellophane and all. It made her want to scream. What about cancer? Her mother laughed at her. "You've got to be cool, baby. They're not yours."

Rain prints the pond now in concentric circles. Before it

begins to pound down in earnest, before the water striders dive for cover in the mud, she scrambles up and goes at a dogtrot along another trail she knows. It leads to the chicken coop of Ted the Wrestler. Ted retired from Stampede Wrestling and now he lives off the land. Ted can call rabbits out of the woods. If he plays his flute, they come and eat from his hand.

She reaches the chicken coop just before the rain lets loose. A person can't go in like the birds do, up the skinny ramp and through the chicken flap. Instead she ducks into the four feet of space under the floor of this pygmy house on stilts. Pushing with her forearms over her head she finds the trapdoor. It falls open inside the coop. She jumps to get her elbows on each side of the hole, then kicks her feet up and rolls onto the straw. The chickens cackle and rustle in greeting. The sweet smell of straw and grain, and the mouldy sour of chicken shit. It's warm and dim. When Ted's away she collects the eggs for him. She knows how to feel between the downy chickens and the prickly straw till she finds an egg, and then the surprise of pulling it out, speckled or brown, cream or pale green.

Shakti lifts the trapdoor with her toe and drops it shut. Looking through the lily flowered window, a relic of some demolished church, she peers down the hill at her parents' land: a tin roofed cabin in a rock-strewn daisy field, surrounded by the dark woods. Through the rain she sees her father and a man running to the woodshed holding coats over their heads. She should just go apologize. But the chicken coop is so warm. Maybe she'll wait for the rain to stop. She finds her favourite chicken, a runty black bantam rooster, and slides her forearm behind his leathery legs, pushing the bird off kilter till he steps back onto her wrist. Wart, she calls him, for the wart on his comb, and for the boy king Arthur in the *Sword in the Stone*. "Look Wart, it's pouring, lucky you're nice and cozy with me." The chicken cocks its pinhead at Shakti with a black and shiny eye. His freckled comb falls sideways over his beak.

Looking out the window, a truck and two cars pull up at the cabin, and then the neighbours arrive, walking in ponchos and carrying casseroles. She'd forgotten. They're hosting a potluck sing-along tonight. River comes out onto the porch and peers through the rain towards the road and then up into the woods. Her mother takes a bowl from a neighbour and holds the door for someone with a guitar. Shakti's stomach growls; maybe she won't wait for the rain to stop after all. But then out of the corner of her eye she sees something black meandering through the bushes. She holds Wart up to look.

"A big old bear Wart. I watched him from a tree today." The bear grubs along, oblivious to the rain and only ten metres away. "Guess we'd better stay put for a little while." She lies on her back in the straw and sits the chicken on her chest, but Wart won't stay put and heads to his roost. Shakti pulls him back. Taking a piece of straw, she splits the last quarter inch of one end with her thumbnail and then fits it over the tip of the bird's beak. Wart's eyes cross as he stares down the centerline at this new prosthetic devise. She chuckles to herself, chicken hypnosis. Planting the transfixed chicken in the straw she gets down a hefty Rhode Island Red. She sets her up with another straw and lays her down beside Wart.

The bear snuffles and roots beneath them now, whuffling up fallen chicken feed with his floppy lips. Shakti shoves some of the straw away so she can see him through the wide cracks. The wiry fur pokes right through a knothole. She touches it with a fingertip. His thick musk wafts into the coop. Just to be on the safe side she sits on the trap door. The bear moves on, but Shakti hypnotizes three more chickens and waits.

The rain pours down, and her stomach aches with hunger. She looks out the window at the woodshed. Her father must still be in there. She just wants to get it over with. Quickly before she changes her mind, she opens the trap door and jumps down. Last thing, she reaches back and plucks five straws off five beaks, and five chickens shake their heads and wake up.

Shakti steps out of the shelter of the trees into the full deluge and walks through the daisies and the woolly leaved mulleins taller than her head. She picks her way around thistles and rocks in her bare feet. The rain soaks her by the time she gets to the wood shed. In the gloom her father and his friend Lou Harlson sit on stumps with the big chopping block between them.

"Hi Daddy." She hesitates a moment. "I came to say I'm sorry." On the chopping block an envelope and a piece of wax paper lie open. She studies the pile of tiny stamps in the center of the paper, each printed with a picture, a star, a lightning bolt, a pirate skull.

"What are those?"

"Keep that little pyromaniac out of here," Lou says, scrabbling at the waxed paper and stuffing it into the envelope.

Her father stands and glowers, grabs her by the arm and drags her behind him stopping in the doorway just under the cover of the eave. The rain pelts down like a curtain inches from her shoulder and splashes mud on her feet. He drops her arm, almost throws it from him.

"This can't happen anymore, Shakti! You can't go around destroying other people's property all the time! I don't know what's happening with kids these days. There's an issue, you know? A basic respect for your elders! There will be a suitable punishment, Shakti. I promise you!" Here he stops. She watches him recede. His eyes grow black and blacker, and then something invisible slides across his face, like the reticulating membrane over the eye of a snake.

"Daddy?" He doesn't hear her but turns and walks into the rain. "Daddy?" she says again to his retreating back. She feels unhinged in the middle. Following him into the rain she goes to find her mother in the cabin.

On the porch she meets Katie Harlson. Katie is twelve, but she still picks her nose in front of anyone and says baby things like "I have to go poo." Yesterday in the orchard they'd been walking, Katie pulling up grasses to chew. Twisting the cat-tailed end of one into a circle, she took another catkin and pushed it back and forth, in and out of the ring. "Sex, sex, sexy…" she'd said, sniggering. Now she corners Shakti against the porch railing, her furry teeth closing in.

"Boy is my dad ever mad at you! He was yelling at your pop. He says you burnt a hundred bucks of his best weed!"

Ah yes, the fat plastic bag in her hand. The stream of green stuff immolating and sparking in the red hole of the wood stove. She'd tossed in the cigarette papers and stuffed in the plastic bag for good measure.

"I don't want to talk about it," Shakti says. She slides along the railing that snags her wet shirt, and twists around the doorframe and into the smoke and crowd of the cabin. Her wet cutoffs, leathery and stiff, threaten to slide off her hipless body. Where is her mother? Through the muddle of lamplit people she finally spots her in the corner. Conspiring with a friend, she shares a cigarette and giggles. Shakti can't see River anywhere. At the table she fills a bowl with brown rice and tofu curry, then squeezes through the crowd to the back room where her parents sleep. A ladder leads up and she climbs it one handed. Crawling onto the floor of the attic she closes another trap door behind her and shuts out the party.

She's alone beneath the pelting rain on the galvanized roof. Shakti walks hunched over so she won't crack her head. In the west dormer her canvas sleeping bag lies stretched in front of the bug-screened window, her chest of treasures at its feet.

She eats as fast as she can in her clammy clothes. Dropping the empty bowl on the floor, she extricates herself from the Guatemalan embroidered top, kicks out of the cutoffs and crawls naked into the sleeping bag. With her knees clutched to her chest she rubs her goose bumpy legs and icy feet. Her teeth chatter. But deep inside she still holds heat, and eventually it begins to collect. It pools in the sleeping bag and finally tips her into warmth. She tries to push away her father's slipping face, the unseen coagulation and collapse of tiny vessels in his brain, the smoke filling her mother's lungs.

The rain drums down and the tympani lulls her. She pretends she is very high up in a great waving fir tree and that she needs no one. And the animals come to her. They come like a parade, radiating sunlight. Silver, and orange, and red and green. Friday dancing with a mane of rippling water. The iridescent beetle as big as a goat. Ted the Wrestler's pigment bright rabbits, huge, softly clucking downy-breasted hens. And ambling along at the very back comes the bear, his fur gold-tipped against the light. Shakti waves to them from her perch. The bear stretches his paws up the trunk to her, raking the bark with his claws. He reaches and waits. Shakti climbs down to him, onto his powerful back, and he carries her off into the dark forest of sleep.

Murdy

Murdoch writhes.

"No go! No go! Want swing!" he bellows. His flannelette blanket twists around his neck as he flails against the stroller seatbelt. Half the blanket falls into the muck on the sidewalk but Moira keeps rolling desperate for home, all the while the rattling dysfunctional Wal-Mart wheel eats up the blanket with enthusiasm. The sudden torsion folds Murdoch efficiently in half. From between his mud smeared corduroy knees, he shouts at the sidewalk. For thirty seconds Moira stands and watches the fluctuating shades of red pulsate in his ears, the screams so lusty she knows his airway is by no means compromised.

"Jesus fucking Christ," she says and sits down on the sidewalk. She rolls onto her knees and gets her head down so that she can look up into the little claret face clashing so violently with his orange hair. "Baby, it's okay. You got tangled up."

Murdoch opens his eyes and looks at her from under one knee. He roars again, but then stops.

"Upside down!" he says in a husky voice, and Moira can't help laughing, her forehead pressed into the gritty sidewalk.

"I'll get you out, just a sec." She tilts the stroller towards her lifting the tangled wheel. Rotating it backwards she unravels the muddy flannel. Murdoch sits up with the blanket dangling around his neck like a soiled napkin, a disgruntled drunken earl. The blood fades form his face and he turns back into a baby.

"Baba?" he asks.

Moira rubs the dirt off her forehead and looks through the diaper bag on the back of the stroller, but he's already drained the bottle of milk. She should have brought two. What was she thinking? If she had plugged him in just before he lost it, the predictable tantrum would never have happened. He'd have fallen asleep part way through the bottle and she could have just carried him inside and laid him on the bed. She keeps digging through the bag. He has to nap so she can get to work. Desperate times call for desperate measures and she finds a half empty bottle of Nestea of uncertain age. She unscrews Murdoch's bottle and rinses the dregs of the milk out with the sweet tea, dumping it out on the grass, and then fills it the rest of the way up.

"Dis yummy for Murdy," she says. "Good juice." She hands him the bottle and he sucks with focus. Now with the lulling rattle of the stroller, in the fifteen-minute walk home he'll fall asleep. She will get two hours, maybe three, to finish the design drawings for the Lieberman house and then email them to Jonathon. All she needs is more coffee. Moira got up this morning at the dark and ungodly hour of four to chew through as many of the design changes as possible. Murdoch's ear infection threw her off her schedule, rendering Jonathon increasingly antsy.

She walks and watches Murdoch's cheeks flex in and out with each suck. Soon the rhythm will slow; his head will nod to the side, the nipple slip from his mouth. The sun warms her back, robins sing in the flowering crab apple trees. Running him at the park had been a good idea; he was tired and ready for a nap now. The elusive work/life balance hovers almost within her reach. Tomorrow the three of them will sleep in.

Moira walks the last block along the river pathway and then pushes the red button at the Sixteenth Avenue crosswalk. The cars stop, and she rolls forward, tilting the stroller on its back wheels to get it over the curb. Murdoch's freckled jowly face looks up at her, his eyes immense and blue, and open.

"Go sleep Murdy!" she says.

"Good juice. More?" He holds the bottle up to her, his forehead wrinkling in supplication.

"That's it buddy! All gone."

By the time they reach the bungalow Murdoch points at birds and dogs, trucks and cats and shouts their names like a little dope fiend on speed. He bounds up the front stairs, his soaking diaper hanging low in his overalls. How could Nestea have so much caffeine? Moira's never felt any buzz at all.

She unlocks the front door, folds up the cheap stroller and hangs it from a hook. Murdy jogs around the living room in circles emitting shrill whistles like a European train. She manages to catch him and pull off his muddy

Buster Browns. Her arm around his belly pins him against her chest, but he twists vigorously giving off another whistle and she just manages to clamp him against her side, riding above her hipbone. She holds him there in flight position. If she weren't so tired, she would zoom him around and pretend he was a helicopter or something, but not today. They go to the bedroom that way, Moira hanging on and Murdoch whistling, and she puts him down on the bed careful to not lose her grip or she'll just have to catch him again. Quickly she strips his overalls off, as well as the five-pound urine drenched diaper. Damn, she forgot to grab a dry one. She turns from him for a minute and reaches for the change table. She rotates back too late and watches him take off running laps around her bed.

"Murdy, come here, baby! What was I thinking with the iced tea?"

"Zooming plane, bzzzzz bzzzz bzzzz." She watches his bandy bowlegs, frog legs like his dad's, powerful now from all those Jolly Jumper workouts. His fluffy baby fat belly powers past her on another lap, his little old man butt twinkling as he rounds the bend. On the next rotation past she catches him with the hook of one arm. He smiles at her broadly, tips his hips forward and ejects an arcing stream of pee from his miniscule widdler. She falls back, her shirt soaked. "No! Don't pee on mama!" She pulls the t-shirt over her head and throws it to the floor. In her bra and jeans, with the dry diaper in hand, she leaps on the bed pinning him beneath her and wrestles on the dry diaper. Murdy jackknifes like a fish and laughs. Holding him tight she finds some clean overalls and gets them on too.

"Fuck! This is going to be some day."

"Fuck!" Murdy says.

"Oh no, baby, no! Don't say that." Murdoch's ears prick at the hysteria in her voice.

"Fuck, fuck, fuck, who-whoooo, fuck, fuck, fuck ..." The little train heads for the living room. Moira covers her face with her hands, her fingertips gripping her forehead. What if he says "fuck" at the park in front of Elizabeth? Elizabeth never swears, and Moira suspects she goes to church. She is the only other mother Moira knows. "I *have* to stop swearing," she thinks, but they'd all sworn like sailors at the office, and motherhood offers double the architecture of frustration.

Moira goes to the bathroom and puts the diaper in the diaper pail. She splashes cold water on her face and dries it. In the mirror she inspects the bags under her eyes and the doughy, hopelessly stretched belly. Murdoch resisted confinement in utero pushing with his head and feet with all his might. Her ribcage measures four inches wider now. He'd remodelled her. He literally expanded her internal capacity. Her arms and shoulders have grown bulky and muscular, and even though she only nurses him at night now, her breasts, tripled in size, look like a cartoon of a Viking maiden.

Standing in front of her closet she surveys the old work clothes that no longer fit. The slim charcoal trousers she can't zip up, tissue weight neutral sweaters that strain across her chest and squeeze her arms like sausage casings, crisp, white ironed blouses that Murdoch would destroy in minutes. Instead she pulls on another stretched out post-delivery t-shirt.

She needs something vaguely hip to wear to lunch with Deidre, the other junior at Templeton and Sons. Deidre, who watched, perplexed from across the café table at Vendome, Murdoch nursing under the receiving blanket, and said: "But what do you *do* all day?"

She'd also referred to the noisy toddler at the next table as "a great form of birth control."

Moira realizes that the train sounds have ceased. She rushes into the living room but there's no sign of him. She finds him in the kitchen sitting cross-legged on the table. He climbed up on a chair and now plucks the petals from the Safeway daffodils she bought yesterday. Daffodils are cheap compared to tulips. He smiles at her adoringly as she picks him up and sets him back on the floor.

"Don't go on the table, Murdy. You'll fall off and break your neck!"

"Mama!" he says. "Break your neck! Fuck!"

"Oh no! Murdy ..."

An epiphany strikes as she puts the kettle on to boil.

"Duck?" she says, but he looks at her with suspicion. Too cheerful, she needs to say it with intensity and anger. She tries again: "Puck, Muck, Luck, Stuck!" Good and angrily. Murdoch remains perplexed. "Fuck?"

"Puddle Duck! Hockey Puck! Smuck!" Ah, those rhyming words, how long could his baby memory persist after all? She goes into the study and pushes the power button on the computer. Then she notices the light on the answering machine flashing. She plays the messages. First Lyle's voice, quiet with exhaustion.

"Hi, honey. Uhhh ... Doug's asked me to do his call

tonight because he seems to have the flu. Sorry. I won't see you till tomorrow. How's Murdy? Page me later 'kay?" the buzz of the phone. Next message.

"Hi, Mo. It's Barb. Jeez I'm sorry, it's been awhile. Just wanted to phone and see how things are on the *home front*. Give me a ring!"

Barb. Moira goes back to the kitchen and waits for the kettle to turn off. Murdoch takes all the pots and pans out of a lower cupboard and she lets him go for it. She fills the French press with ground coffee and pours in the boiling water. She and Barb at Sullivan's wedding eating canapés under the apple tree.

"Are you sure about this?"

"About what?"

"The baby."

"Well, I guess I wouldn't say 'sure' is the word. It's more something I feel, I don't know maybe compelled to do? I ..."

"It's just that all the mothers I've worked with at the Bay were kind of, uh, you know, *balmy*."

"What do you mean *balmy*?"

"Out of touch, you know. Stupid really. Neurotic. I'm just wondering if you're sure about this."

"Well, it's a little late now, Barb."

Moira stirs the coffee grounds into the water and eats a banana while she waits for it to brew. She slices up a quarter of another banana and puts it into Murdoch's divided dish with the rabbits. In another section she puts in some cottage cheese and sprinkles it with cinnamon. The meal looks too white, not enough vitamin rich foods.

Moira finds a bag of edamame beans in the freezer, dumps a handful into a strainer and defrosts them under the tap. She tips them into the third compartment of the bowl, looking with approval at their vibrant green, and fills a Sippy cup with milk. In a minute she plunges the coffee. The French roast aroma rises up, and she hopes another cup will help considering her existing caffeine saturation.

Moira turns over the stockpot to make a little table in front of Murdoch and puts his dish with the rubber coated baby spoon beside it. She sits him on an upside-down saucepan and the arrangement pleases him. He tucks into the cottage cheese, then picks up each jade green bean and with his thumb and forefinger and pops it in his mouth. When he is done, she washes him down and carries him to the living room, sitting him on the couch with his Sippy cup.

"Zaboomafoo?"

"Yah, Boom a Foo!" Outside the spring wind wafts, leaves unfurling, and here he'll sit in the stuffy living room watching Netflix. She hadn't intended it to be like this so much of the time, but what else can she do? She releases the latch on a window and cranks it open, then goes to the study with her cup of coffee.

Moira opens the Lieberman House file on CAD, and flips through the changes Jonathon sent her from the last design meeting. She only needs to finish the kitchen. Apparently, Mrs. Lieberman, Janice, decided against the modernist teak cabinetry, and now wants everything French provincial, ah yes, with the addition of a brick pizza oven. Moira draws the fiddly mouldings on the first standard size cabinet door and then copies and pastes them wherever she can. On some non-standard cabinets she has to trim and futz about. She is so tired she keeps making mistakes, but she gets the job done in half an hour and starts switching the pot lights to pendant hurricane style lamps over the island. She draws one lamp after eyeballing the sample in the lighting catalogue, close enough. She glances at the clock. That took twenty minutes. Goddamn, now she has to change the stacked modernist glass tile backsplash to traditional subway tile in a brick layout. Moira deletes the old hatching pattern, looks up brick bond in the pattern menu and tries to insert it into her original outline. The computer whirs, in a minute the new pattern will pop into place. Sometimes computers really were a godsend. Aaah, shit! The computer inserted the brick pattern but at some micro scale. Delete, delete! Finally, she gets the hatching to cooperate and starts working on the beehive pizza oven. No doubt that had been Jonathon's idea, his signature touch being a traditional Rumford masonry fireplace in every possible room, so a wood burning pizza oven was perfectly simpatico.

Originally Moira liked that about him. The efficiency of a Rumford fireplace versus your average modern knock off couldn't be argued with. She appreciated that level of scholarship and interest in history. Today however, Moira can't locate any passion for the detailing of a pizza oven. She scrolls desperately though her file on fireplaces, no pizza ovens. Finally, she just Googles pizza oven images and finds the one Jamie Oliver built in his back yard. She sketches it in roughly in CAD. After all this was just a design drawing. The techs would detail it later.

She sorts through the pile of changes again, checking off the completed ones. Jonathon had been so flexible with all of Murdy's illnesses. He didn't want to lose her, his go-to designer who stayed late, skipped weekends, and did whatever he needed to accommodate a fussy client or his own sudden artistic inspiration. That Christmas Eve for instance, with Jonathon pacing behind her chair demanding a barrel vault detail for a library ceiling. That was between his marriages. He had no one to spend Christmas with anyhow, and Moira knew how to make him laugh.

In the boardroom, sitting with two-month-old Murdoch on her lap, the sunlight turning her and Murdoch's copper hair to gold. She looks down at the baby and brushes the damp curls on his forehead protectively. Jonathon leans forward smiling and stares too long as Murdoch nestles between her new turgid breasts.

"Mother and child," he says. "No wonder there are so many paintings of the Madonna."

"I think I could balance that," Moira says. "One project at a time should be fine."

"Well that settles it then. And when you feel ready you can come back full time."

"Yes. When he's older." Moira stands up. "Good, then I'll start with the Gilman renovation."

"Mama?" Murdoch stands beside her. She glances at the clock, which reads four thirty. He has been watching Zaboomafoo for two hours and exudes a rank odour from his diaper. How long had he been sitting in that? The digestive juice laden crap erodes his baby skin so quickly. She doesn't want him starting another diaper rash.

"I'm sorry, buddy. Let's go get you changed." She takes his small hand and they walk into the bedroom. The Nestea seems to be wearing off because he lies there patiently on the change table while she cleans him up.

"Mama, play Murdy?"

"Oh baby, I'm almost done and then we can play. It's such a beautiful day. You should be outside. I know! I'll put your paint easel out on the back deck and you can paint, okay? Mama can watch you through the window."

"Paint," Murdoch says. "Hose? Sandbox?"

"Sure, sweetie, it's a warm day. You can have the hose." She puts on his sunhat and sets the easel up outside with the five jars of tempera paint and pins a big piece of paper up. "Do you want the hose first?"

"Yah! In sandbox."

"Okay. Don't make too big a lake. Here, I'll get your plastic animals." When he settles in the sandbox digging out holes and channels for the water, she goes back to the kitchen and gets another cup of now cold coffee. She sits back down at her desk and opens the window, so she can hear him. The phone rings.

"Moira?"

"Oh, hi Jonathon."

"I just need to know how close we are. Janice wants to move the meeting up till tomorrow. We've been putting her off too long. I can't keep stalling her."

"I know. I'm really sorry. Murdoch's ear infection totally threw me off. No one was sleeping, but I'm on top of the design drawings now. I just finished all the kitchen changes."

"Well, she faxed me some additional changes, and we'll need them by tomorrow at eleven."

"What sort of changes?"

"The façade of the house actually. She wants to move it more toward Georgian traditional."

"Jesus Oliver, Georgian traditional? It's a modernist house; the kitchen is just a little detour. There's no way I can get that done for tomorrow, I need more notice than that."

"Janice has really been very patient, Moira. We have to accommodate her now. Actually, we've *all* been very patient, Moira." His voice takes on that peevish tone.

"I can't tell you how much I appreciate that, Jonathon ..."

"There was colic with the Gilman house ..."

"Yes."

"Croup with the Didsbys," he says, warming up. "Teething all through the MacNeil residence, and then the Watsons and the god forsaken ear infections started. When is it going to end, tell me that?"

"I ..."

His voice quiets. "Tell me that, Moira, when is it going to end?"

"I don't know," she says, and then finally. "I guess it doesn't."

"You know how I feel about you, Moira. You're a very talented designer and we've been a great team. Can't you find some childcare? Where is this husband of yours anyhow? Can't he help you out more?"

"No. Not with the rotations he's doing and the call he has to carry. We're living on student loans." Pleading now.

"And I know you won't consider full time work and daycare."

There is nothing she can say.

"This is hard for me, Moira, but I need you to transfer the file to Deidre. She can make the changes I want tonight. I've been very flexible."

Her throat seizes up.

"Is that okay, Moira? You'll do that?"

"Yes, Jonathon," she manages to say. "I'll transfer it to Deidre."

"I'm sorry. No one is sorrier about this than I am. Come in to the office in a few days and Connie will tally up your time sheet." Click as his receiver goes down, the buzz of the phone. Moira sits staring out the window at the sandbox.

The sandbox. The hose still runs, and the sandbox sits filled to the brim. Where is Murdoch? She runs out of the study to the back door of the kitchen. In the fenced yard he couldn't have gone anywhere, but she scans wildly and can't find him.

"Murdoch!"

"Mama?" his little piping voice answers from behind the garden shed. Moira stumbles across the yard, still thinking of the phone call. When she reaches the corner of the shed and sees him, she screams. Murdoch has somehow turned black, as though singed, as though burnt to charcoal.

His blue eyes get very big in his smudged face.

"Paint!" He holds up the black jar of Tempra in one hand and a dripping brush in the other.

"My God, what have you done?" She starts to laugh. He must have taken off his t-shirt and overalls and systematically painted, slathered, every place he could reach with glistening black.

"Oh, my goodness, Murdoch. What are we going to do?" She stares at him while he goes back to slowly anointing his belly with the paintbrush.

"Buddy," she says finally, "come on, it's tubby time."

In the bathroom she runs the tap till the water warms up and then flips the lever for the hand shower. The paint, already drying to a matte finish, cracks and flakes off of his skin. She picks him up and puts him in the tub.

"Stand still, Murdy. I've got to hose you down." When she gets most of the paint off, she rinses out the tub and then starts it filling. She pulls off her own clothes and climbs in with him.

"What are we going to do, Murdy? Mama is officially unemployed." She stares at his belly and realizes that the paint stained him grey wherever it touched. She gets some shampoo and tries to soap it off, but although the stain lightens, he looks like he's been bruised all over. My God if the public health nurse saw this, or heaven forbid Elizabeth, they'd call Child Welfare. She fills an empty shampoo bottle and lets the water run over his shoulders to wash away the soap. Tears meander hot trails down her cheeks. She and Murdy, and the next six years till Lyle's done residency stretch before her like an endless tunnel. She covers her face with her hands and tries not to scare him by making any noise.

At the front of the tub, Murdy crouches, holding the

empty shampoo bottle under the stream of water. She feels the bottle touch her head, and the warmth rivulets around her ears and down her chin. She lifts her face to the water.

"Washing Mama. Soap up." He pours an unknown quantity of shampoo on her head, and his little fingers go to work patting and poking her hair. Tenderly, while she keeps her eyes tight shut, he strokes the bubbles over her face. "Nice and clean now," he says, and she stays that way for a long time, hypnotized by the fleeting touches of his hands and his erratic baby breaths of concentration. "Wash it off," and the rough plastic lip of the empty bottle rest on the bridge of her nose, her forehead. When he's finished, he focuses on motoring a plastic goat around in green rowboat. Moira lies back in the tub and rinses the soap from her hair.

They towel down. She puts Murdoch in a diaper and a clean sleeper. In the kitchen she makes two peanut butter sandwiches and pours them each some milk. They eat sitting side by side in the scattered cookware, Moira on an overturned stockpot and Murdy perched on a mixing bowl. The clock says ten past seven. She wants to page Lyle but is just too weary.

"Are you tired, Buddy?"

"Go bed," he says.

In the bedroom Moira strips off the grimy sheets, picks up all the dirty clothes and then throws the lot down the basement stairs. Then she goes to the study and opens an email to Deidre. She mistypes twice but finally attaches the CAD file for the Lieberman house. Send.

She returns to Murdoch and makes up the bed with

clean linen. Opening the window to the breeze she lets the bathrobe drop and slips naked between the sheets. Pulling his warm sleeper clad body in tight, she tucks him under her chin.

He twists to see her face. "*Duck! Hockey Puck!*" he says fiercely.

"Oh *no*, Murdy! Don't say *that*, don't say *Hockey Puck*!" Murdoch sighs with contentment and rotates back. "Mum, mum, mum," he murmurs into her chest, then finds a nipple and latches on.

Outside the robins flute their evening song. The gauzy Ikea curtains lift in the wind. She drifts. She holds onto Murdy and swims in a dark sea. He is so buoyant, so solid. He begins to grow till she is the small one clinging to his back. His turquoise eyes rimmed with their white lashes just above the azure water, his copper curls blow back in the wind. She feels the kick, the power of the hypo-drive starting up deep within him. His lips buzz on the margin of the water, and the bubbles surge back in their wake.

"Who-whoooo!" That shrill whistle. She locks her arms through the straps of his overalls and buries her face in the soft nap of the corduroy. She knows if she can only hold on, she will not sink beneath the waves.

Thirty-third Street

Her rule for the To-Do List is "the hardest thing first." So, informing the school that Rilla contracted head lice that one time, or purging the basement laundry room after the sewer back up, or mundane horrors like organizing all the paper work at tax time. But now that the twins have started grade one and she finally has time, the hardest thing is simply to begin, to walk into her garage studio and get the damn brush on the canvas.

Today is such a day, but when she does, Mariah finds a dead cat lying on the concrete floor. The way it reclines for a weird moment reminds her of her nude modeling days as an art student in college. She shrieks and jumps back, clutching her plaid flannel-painting shirt around her. The cat lying in a patch of sunlight is so clearly not sleeping. Its body contorts backwards in an acute arch and the lips pull away in a grimace. Watery vomit lies in a puddle beside its head.

"Oh my God," Mariah says. "I don't own a cat!" And her eyes scan wildly. The north-facing window stands open, left that way to air out the studio after she'd cleaned the brushes with turpentine last night. The cat is massive, black with white paws and a white bib extending up its throat and over the top lip of his jowls. The white upper lip, the long white whiskers, the little black goatee on his chin, and then the sheer size of him make him unmistakable. Louise's cat Stache. Louise lives across the street in a tiny stucco bungalow behind a high manicured hedge. She is ninety-two. This four-block stretch of Thirty-third Street resonates with that hedge, manicured, immaculate, and populated thickly with retirees.

Mariah and Liam's place, a blazingly white Victorian row house they recently acquired when the Edelsons moved to assisted living, has exploded at the hands of their three children. A trampoline, and skateboards, bikes, chalk drawings all over the sidewalk, dandelions, and strange modernist sculptures in the front yard.

She sinks to her knees and examines him. She sees swirls of colour in the cat's vomit, Barium Yellow, Cobalt Violet, a swipe of Scheele's green on Max's white bib. The pads of his paws show violet and yellow and red.

A trail of smudged footprints leads from her palette on the counter, down and across the floor. He must have licked the paint on his paws and poisoned himself in the night while they slept. As if the chaos of their yard isn't enough, now she is responsible for poisoning the venerable cat of the street's oldest resident.

Mariah kneads her forehead frantically. What to do? Louise seems so fragile and ancient, and Stache she assumes must be very important to her. She searches in her mind for some rule of conduct, some suggestion from Miss Manners on the etiquette of returning poisoned cats. All that she comes up with is her own rule: do the hardest thing first. But before that she thinks she'll phone her husband. Her cell phone must be in the kitchen, so she goes to retrieve it. Shaking a bit, she scrolls to his work number. He will know what to do; he usually does.

"Department of History, Main Office, Cheryl speaking."

"Hi Cheryl, is Liam still in that meeting? I really need to talk to him."

"Actually, they haven't started yet. I'll just put you through to the boardroom." There was a space of dead air and then Liam picks up.

"What? Run that by me again. You killed a cat?"

"Well not on purpose! Louise …"

"Who's Louise?"

"The old lady across the street. It's her cat. He's lying here, and it looks like it was a horribly painful death. What do I do? I have to tell Louise."

"How toxic is the paint?" She hears Liam shuffling through papers.

"I don't know, but he got some Scheele's Green, and I think that has arsenic in it. There's some lead in some of the others, for sure."

"Well, Hun, hmmm, I've got to get organized for this meeting, but it seems awfully quick for a poisoning. You know, the Romans drank from lead pipes for decades, and they still managed to dominate the world. Oh, and the hatters, sure they went crazy with the mercury, but they made a lot of hats first."

"Well, he's definitely *dead*, Liam."

"I don't know, honey, I'm sure you'll think of the right thing to say. You always do. I've got to go over some stuff here before the Dean comes in to barbecue me. I'll see you tonight okay?"

"That's it? That's all you can say?"

"Well, just check to be sure he's really dead."

She goes back into the studio and stares at the cat's pitiful face. The lips have slipped back, covering his teeth, and his whiskers stir a little. He must still be breathing. Maybe Liam is right. Mariah pulls off her painting shirt and finds an orange crate under the worktable. She creeps up to the cat. How do you touch so much agony?

"Okay, kitty. I'm going to wrap you up and put you in a box, okay? We're going to the doctor."

Mariah gingerly covers him with the shirt. Then she slides her hands and the flannel underneath him like tucking a sheet around a mattress. The big old tom weighs maybe fifteen pounds. With her arms under him now she slowly stands up. Then he starts to leak. Something wet from his head, and he pees all over her other forearm. He jackknifes, and she almost drops him, just managing to lay him in the orange crate. She waits for any further movement then dashes into the house for her purse.

In the driveway the gimlet eye of Madge Pickers over the fence stops her short. The Pickers' fence is chain link woven through with white vinyl strips on the diagonal, over the top of which Madge keeps them in steady surveillance. Now Madge scrutinizes the box. Ever since their midsummer's eve party last year, when Liam re-enacted his family's Danish custom of burning a witch (in effigy of course), Mrs. Pickers, a devout Baptist, has viewed them with suspicion. Mariah offered her lox on Melba toast and explained the Danish folk custom of burning a scarecrow witch as a symbolic cleansing of past sins, the welcoming of a fresh new year. But Mrs. Pickers brusquely refused the proffered glass of Aquavit and muttered something about "heathen goings on" before turning on her heel, the screen door clicking closed behind her.

"Good morning, Mrs. Pickers!" Mariah says, sounding as wholesome and upstanding as possible.

"Mrawww," the cat says, very loudly. He lurches into a sitting position, his black head escaping the flannel shirt. Drool runs out of his mouth like water, and he collapses back into the box with a whimper.

"I didn't know you had a cat," Mrs. Pickers says. "A *black* cat."

"Oh, it's quite hard to explain," Mariah says, prickly sweat breaking out on her chest. "He's actually not mine, but he's very sick. I'm just getting him to the vet, so I've really got to run." Mrs. Pickers almost says something, restrains herself, but then she bites.

"Mr. Pickers told me I had to tell *you*, that he is *quite* fed up with the dandelion situation in your driveway. If you don't take care of them by the weekend, he'll just come over and take care of them *himself*!"

"Oh dear. I am so sorry. They do spread, don't they? I'll try to take care of them today, but really, I must run. So sorry!"

Mariah manages to get the car door open and lays the box on the passenger seat. She backs out of the driveway. The cat was shitting now, and the car fills with the stink. She drives as fast as she can to the vet clinic they used before they put their old dog down, and Dr. Belfast squeezes her in between appointments. He holds Max in his large hands. He listens to his heart and palpates his belly.

"Oil paints, you say?"

"Yes, I'm afraid he jumped right onto my wet palette and then he licked it off his paws in the night."

"Well, he shows all the classic signs of poisoning, salivation, lacrimation, urination and defecation. But oil paints wouldn't do that. He'd have to eat a lot of it and it would take weeks. This looks to me like some type of herbicide. An organophosphate probably."

"Oh, what a relief!" Mariah flumps into a chair. "I didn't do this to him then?"

"No, he must have gotten into something else. Lucky he's a big fellow. His heart rate is too slow, so I'll give him a dose of Atropine and put him on IV fluids. Then we'll just have to wait and hope. You'll need to leave him here and we'll see if he can metabolize the stuff. In a day or two we'll know one way or another." Dr. Belfast holds him drooping against his forearm. "He's an intact male, big old Tomcat. You don't see that too often now a days. Your neighbour's cat, you say?"

On the drive home she revises the to-do list. She needs to tell Louise. You can't just pretend nothing happened. If the cat should die, Louise deserves at least the chance to say goodbye.

Turning too quickly into her driveway she doesn't

immediately spot the man standing there. Luckily, he is dressed from neck to ankles in blazing orange. As she slams her foot on the brake, she realizes it is not a city worker. It's Mr. Pickers. He bends over, squirting the dandelions in the cracked asphalt with a plastic spray bottle. The car skids to a halt a metre from his broad backside. Mr. Pickers straightens up, the orange coveralls he wears for yard work straining over his massive beer belly. He glowers at her officiously from between his receding chin and a greasy comb over. *For all the world*, Mariah thinks, *as if it were* his *driveway*. The poisoned cat still contorting in the back of her mind, Mariah gets out of the car and finds she has slammed the door.

"Mr. Pickers," she says. "You are on *my* property without permission, and you have no right to be spraying toxic chemicals around my yard!"

By the time she finishes the sentence, she is shouting. It is very satisfying, although she knows in a distant way she will regret it shortly. Nonetheless, with what feels like fire blowing out of her ears, she leans forward and wrests the spray bottle from Mr. Pickers' pudgy hand.

"This is *toxic*, Mr. Pickers. This is *poison*, and it is no doubt what is killing Louise's cat Stache right now! I just took him to the vet and he confirmed that he is suffering from acute insecticide poisoning. How much of this stuff have you been spraying around?" She shakes the spray bottle under his nose.

Mr. Pickers stares at her. He straightens his shoulders and thrusts his belly forward like the prow of a battleship. And then he does something totally unexpected.

"Mariah," he says. "I do believe you've had a bad morning." And he smiles at her.

She deflates. She feels like weeping.

"Yes, how did you know? The cat was really a terrible shock, he got into my studio last night, and he is in such pain …"

"Well, don't you worry, dear." He gently takes the spray bottle back. "This is Round-Up. It's a herbicide, not a pesticide, and it's totally safe for animals. The garden centre assured me it is nontoxic. You know I've got my little dog to think about, and my pigeons."

"Oh Mr. Pickers. I feel like a fool, yelling at you like that. Liam says I have a short fuse. I'm really sorry!"

"Well, it *is* your yard. I thought I'd just slip in while you were away and take care of these dandelions for you. But I should have asked." He smiles again. Comb over aside, he has kindly eyes. "You know, the Missus gets feisty with too much on her mind." He glances over his shoulder at the mint green bungalow. "Though she's got a heart of gold underneath. You can't find a woman more loyal than Madge."

"I feel awful, Mr. Pickers. I so dread this. I have to go over now and tell Louise that her cat poisoned himself with some sort of pesticide. The vet says he might survive because he's such a big fellow. But there's no guarantee. I don't know what to say to her."

"Well, I'll go with you," Mr. Pickers says. "We've lived here for forty years so I know her pretty well."

"Oh, thank you, Mr. Pickers!"

"Call me Jim, Mariah. We're neighbours after all."

Together, they cross the street. It is almost eleven now, on a beautiful Monday at the end of June. Just over the hedge she glimpses the sparse silvery down on Louise's pink scalp, shimmering and waving a little in the breeze. Mr. Pickers opens the waist-high metal gate with curlicues on top and holds it for Mariah to go through. She realizes she never knew what lay behind the hedge, and now she gasps. Wide flowerbeds run down both the east and west sides of the handkerchief-sized yard, leaving only room for a mower-wide strip of grass and a path to the front door, each bed an explosion of roses in every shade of saffron and coral, pink and crimson and white. Louise is a tiny woman whose body has collapsed irrevocably over the years into an increasingly pyramidal form. She wears a faded flowered dress and an old man's cardigan. Her calves run thick and ankle-less to her leather loafers bruised with varicose veins, the skin dry and cracked. Leaning over the roses she plucks off dead leaves and strokes the blossoms with arthritic swollen claws. She doesn't turn when they come in.

"Morning, Louise!" Mr. Pickers says loudly and cheerfully. Louise straightens up and looks at them, her face creases into a smile.

"Your roses have never put on a better show, Louise! You remember Mariah, don't you? She moved into the Edleson house."

"Oh yes," she says, "The Edleson house. How are you liking it, dear? Isn't this a lovely day?"

Mariah steps up beside Louise to admire the flowers. "I never could grow roses," she says. "How do you do this? They're quite amazing!"

The old lady pulls a rusty pair of scissors from the cardigan pocket and nips off a dead flower. "You have to baby them, dear. Fertilize, water twice a week. This year the aphids have been so terrible! I had to spray them yesterday, but I don't think I got them all. I'll spray them again today. But I can't find my Malathion! You can't get it anymore you know, the good stuff." She grins at them. "The garden centre says they won't sell it anymore, so I *must* find it. It's so frustrating. I can't get anything done!" She looks around her garden. "Now I can't even find my cat. You haven't seen Stache, have you? He didn't come home for breakfast."

Mariah opens her mouth, but Louise goes on.

"I was wanting your help, Jim," she says. "Come inside, there was something I needed to give you. For the life of me I don't remember now …"

They stand in the tiny musty entry on a tattered doormat while she clatters around the kitchen. On the boot shelf below a row of coat hooks, both Mariah and Mr. Pickers see it at the same time, a brown glass bottle the size and shape of a whiskey flask. The stained label reads: "Malathion." They look at each other. Mariah picks it up.

"Here," Mr. Pickers says. Mariah hands it to him and he slides it into one of the vast pockets of the orange coveralls.

"Oh, I found it!" Louise calls from the kitchen. She comes out to the entry holding a Pyrex bowl. "I think this must be Madge's. Will you return it to her?"

"Well of course I will, Louise. And don't you worry about Stache. He's probably just in the hill tom catting around."

"Yes," Louise says, chuckling. "He likes to check in on his lady friends!"

"Well, I wanted to ask you, Louise, if you want any of our Nanking cherries this year for making jelly? Madge has more than she can handle." Mr. Pickers talks over his shoulder as he takes Mariah by the elbow and propels her gently out the door and down the path.

"Oh, that would be nice! I'll come by and get them later, once I've dealt with these aphids." They leave her muttering to herself and shuffling about the garden. The gate clicks shut behind them.

Thursday morning, the twins and Rilla eat their breakfast. She makes their lunches, kisses them, and sends them off to the bus stop. Now sitting and drinking her coffee pencil in hand, she looks at the to do list. Then she stands up, takes her purse and keys and goes to the car. She drives to the clinic.

In an hour she is back sitting in the driveway, parked right behind her house so as not to be seen from the street. On the seat beside her, in a cardboard cat carrier, Stache yowls his discontent. She takes the carrier out of the car and sets it on the pavement. Mariah pulls the handles apart to open the top and lifts out all his elastic heaviness.

Smudges of paint remain on his chin and paws. She wonders what Louise will make of them. Mariah sets him on his feet. Holding him still for a moment between her forearms, she gives him a good scratch around the neck.

The deep throttle purr starts up. "Go home," she says, and releases him. After a few figure eights around her ankles, he heads with his purposeful heavy tread down the driveway towards breakfast. Mariah watches as he squeezes through the gap between the hedge and Louise's gate. The white tipped tail vanishes with a twitch.

Mariah stands in the driveway and surveys her yard. The sun glitters in the spear-shaped leaves of the old willow and illuminates the silver spheres of the dandelions in the driveway. She hears Mrs. Waller down two houses, asking her husband to turn up the sprinkler, and from the corner she can just make out a baby crying from that new family. What was their name? Chang maybe? Next-door Jim starts up his lawn mower. Mariah walks up the back stairs and lets herself into the kitchen for more coffee. It seems a propitious day for working in the studio.

Walking Leonard

I walk Leonard in the derelict land between the highway and the trailer park. Paths run here, through groves of aspen and scrub cottonwood, curving down coulis and around cattail sloughs, through high tawny grasses and silver sage. I strip the bobbly flowers off the sage and rub them into my palms, breathe in the scent and run it through my hair.

In the eighties they tried to develop this land. They brought in bulldozers and backhoes and tore up the prairie by its roots. But seeds and shoots can't be so dissuaded, and the native plants came back. They hold their own now against the thistles and the dandelions. Today, in September, golden rod and purple asters bloom again in something approaching abundance.

In the centre of this wasteland you stumble on what looks like the set for a Mad Max movie. It's an old construction waste dump. Twisted rebar, broken slabs of concrete and sections of sewer pipe I can almost stand up in. But even here the poplar seedlings and yellow clematis insinuate and interlace. And the bulldozers never could touch the space in the wasteland, so vast, or the light. The wind shakes the trees and turns them to silver in the sun;

it swirls up and out all the way to the blue Rocky Mountain horizon.

I shouldn't walk here. My parents worry about crack heads and transients off the highway, biker guys from the trailer park, and coyotes. Supposedly they've eaten a few Peek-a-poos. There is a story of a trailer park dog that took himself for a walk in January. A winter-famished coyote, tired of filling up on freeze-dried rose hips, stalked him through the scrub. The dog high tailed it for home, the coyote behind him all the way, heading for the chain link fence beside the trailer park road. The dog just reached the gate when the driver of the number forty saw him. The bus slowed down, the driver opened the door, and the dog jumped in. He rode away laughing, leaving the coyote behind on the frozen road in a cloud of diesel exhaust.

That is the sort of thing that can happen up here in the wasteland. This is the place where I met the man I call "Jesus."

Leonard is a Weimaraner. He has a coat like grey silk. He is long and aristocratic and neurotic as hell. My mother Celine bought him from a breeder in the States because his father won some Weimaraner championship and she wanted to best her sister Cecile. Cecile bought a purebred Standard Poodle from a local breeder. My mother comes from a family of four sisters, and although they're nearing sixty, they still remember exactly who stole whose boyfriend, who got the highest marks in every grade, who won some puppet making contest and who only got third. If you put those four in a room together, you can cut the air with a knife.

On Saturday my mother kind of vibrates butter onto toast as we discuss my various options for university. In September I'll start grade twelve, so I need to apply to universities now. Leonard lies on my feet also vibrating. He can't help it, he always does. It keeps my feet warm, but the nervous tick under my left eyebrow starts up and marks time with the kitchen clock.

"Clarice," she says, "your grade point average is ninety-eight percent in an International Baccalaureate program, *while* making provincials with your swimming. Don't forget your IQ came in at 135. You'll need a copy of the psychologist's academic assessment. Oh, and include your volunteer work at the Women's Shelter and all your coaching, and the City Youth Commission on Inclusivity. Oh yes and don't forget The Young Canadians. You are *not*"—buffing the glasses as she takes them from the dishwasher—"you are *not* applying to UBC or Nova Scotia Tech, for the love of *God*!"

"But UBC is well respected and the botany department actually ..."

My father comes into the kitchen in his running gear. He trains for a marathon every year. This time he's doing the ING New York City Marathon in November.

"Botany! Good God Harold, *botany*?"

"Your mother's right, buddy." He punches me gently on the shoulder. "Don't sell yourself short. Who's my little shooting star? By the way, I'm going to drop in at the hospital after my run." He kisses my mother on the cheek. My father heads up internal medicine at the Foothills Hospital, which means I mainly see him running out the door.

"Don't forget dinner tonight with the Barrys at the club," my mother says. "They said seven thirty." Then she turns to me: "Will you come? Peter will be there ..."

The Barrys have a son called Peter. At a swim club end of season party, after my first ever martini, I ended up kissing Peter in the walk-in-fridge of the Sheraton banquet room. I am unclear how this came about. Peter wants to be a litigation lawyer. He won at Nationals in the Butterfly last year and loves to golf. He leaves for Harvard in September. He looked so good in the fridge that night I am ashamed to admit, purely due to a certain silky turgidity. Peter is the closest thing to a walking talking penis you'll ever meet. Tonight, I would rather saw off my leg without anesthesia then go face to face with Peter and his parents at the Winter Club.

"No! Uh, I mean, I've got to work on these applications. I'll take Leonard out for a walk."

"But *not* in that dangerous field!" she says to my dad, who's mixing protein powder into a glass of orange juice. "If we still lived in Oakville, I wouldn't have to worry about her. She could just go to River Park. And it *drives* me how Cecile says '*Bowness*'."

"How does she say '*Bowness*'?"

"I don't know. There's an undertone. Just because she lives in Rideau Park!"

My father knocks back the orange juice slurry.

"This is a two-million-dollar home on the Bow River,

Celine, and I can run to work. Cecile can think what she likes."

"I'll just take Leonard to Bowmont Park and throw the ball for him. There's always tons of people there."

My mother holds onto the counter, doing alternating sets of leg lifts and calf raises.

"Not till you get your applications done, Clarey. I absolutely insist on Harvard and Brandeis at a bare minimum. Oh, I'm going to Lou Lou today. Why don't I pick you up a few new hoodies?"

"My old ones just got comfortable!"

"They're starting to pill. You look scruffy."

"Okay," I say. I don't think I've ever worn out a piece of clothing or had a favourite old anything. My walk-in closet looks like a boutique, all the clothes arranged in graduated colour, precision folded and stacked. A pursuit of my mother's when I'm swimming, or volunteering, or at school.

In June, during exam week, I go up to the field on a Friday. Around two in the afternoon on a hot still day, just the buzz of insects and the distant drone of the highway. If you're up there before supper on weekdays, or mornings on weekends, lots of people from the trailer park walk their dogs. The funny thing is the conversations, just polite dog-park-ese with a few more pit bulls thrown in. You talk about breeds, and dog names, and health issues. There's a protocol to it. Who knows what people are going through in their personal lives; you all smile at each other and talk about hip dysplasia in German Shepherds. You could have the same conversation in any off leash in the city, even Rideau Park.

But up here at two in the afternoon on a weekday I own the place. I like to walk alone. Not because of Leonard, of course. If anything happened, I'd have to rescue *him*, not the other way around. But I'm at one with the wind and the light and the plants up here. I'm like a rabbit, good at camouflage.

I follow the path down the hill through some willow. We circle around the bottom slough and I try to get Leonard to retrieve a stick from the water, but he doesn't like to get his feet wet. We follow the path parallel to the highway, then up and around another rise to the top where the path cuts through a field of chest high waving grass and wild roses.

And then at the Mad Max dumping ground a man steps out between two piles of scrap concrete. I jump. His long hair falls to his waist, grey and brown and verging on dreadlocks. He looks like Jesus after way too much sun exposure on the cross. I'm annoyed at my heart, whackity-whacking under my collarbones. Leonard vibrates against my leg and then he pees on my left runner.

"Hi," the man says.

Six dogs emerge from the scrap concrete behind him. A small Husky darts and dashes at Leonard. Leonard never plays with anyone, but to my amazement he starts chasing the Husky in ever widening circles. Jesus says: "Lucy still needs a lot of exercise."

"She's a Husky?"

"No, a Samoyed. The runt."

I stand still and wait for the man to pick a path, but he seems in no hurry. He just stands there watching the dogs.

"Can I walk with you? I need to tire Lucy out and she doesn't play so much with my old dogs."

"Uh, okay. I'm heading back to the car." I rotate on my heel, no way in hell I'll take the isolated loop that runs beside the Douglas firs. We start walking. From the corner of my eye I watch his spattered work boots and canvas overalls. He looks wiry and ripped under his clothes and I can't decide on his age by his worn-out face. Quiet settles around us, not a breath of wind.

He tells me the names of the other five dogs. A stumpy black-lab-cross with a lot of fatty growths under his skin. Her name is Trouble and she's nine. Jessie, his overweight grey-muzzled golden retriever walks by his knee. Then there's the Samoyed Lucy, and three other little nondescript mongrels. Jesus, and half a dozen disciples.

"Jessie's twelve now. I take him to all my jobs with me. The people always love him. The last house I did, the family really liked him. They tried to buy him for three hundred bucks. But I need his company."

"What do you do?"

"I'm a framer."

He walks too slowly, so where the path narrows, I go in front to set the pace. In the field with the roses we can walk abreast again, and he slows back down. He talks about coyotes.

"I've never run into one," I say, "but I've heard stories."

"Oh, they're here all right. A big gal's got a den in the bush near my place." He points, and I squint at the far edge of the trailer park. "I've seen her sniffing around. She can smell the meat."

"The meat?"

"Yeah, I like to feed them a raw meat diet, it keeps them fit. I buy it bulk and keep it in my freezer. I chop it up with an axe on a block in the yard, so that's what the coyote gal's smelling."

"Oh!" I study the not so fit dogs milling through the grass ahead of us.

"Some people put out poison bait for them, but what if my dogs got into it, eh?"

"I never thought of that. Do you mean it's up here? Leonard stays pretty close but he'll eat anything."

"Well that was some years ago. I just chase them off with my bike personally. It works pretty good."

"Really?"

"Yeah. You don't want coyotes getting too friendly."

"No, I guess not."

We come to the eight-foot chain link fence. The Tiny trailer yards back onto it, and one of them is his. He's cut a gate into the chain link and built a bench that sits on the wild side. I remember seeing him now, sitting there in the evening drinking a beer.

"This is my favourite place for a beer," he says.

He opens the gate to go in, and that idiot Leonard dashes ahead of him and starts running loops with Lucy around the back yard.

"Leonard! Come back here!"

"He smells the meat." Jesus tips his chin towards the stump with its embedded axe. "You can just come in and grab him if you want." I smile but I don't move. Eventually he herds him out and I grab him by the collar.

"Thanks a lot, Leonard," I say, and we head for the car.

"What do *you* think, Harold?" We're sitting down for Cecile's prescribed Sunday togetherness dinner. Tonight, rack of lamb, green beans and Potatoes Anna. Peaches with kirsch and crème fraiche for desert.

"Well, I can't see straight sciences, Clarice, certainly not botany. What would you do with botany? Dentistry I guess at the very least. Law, medicine, of course. Engineering leaves me a little cold but you do excel at math. I'd take architecture over engineering. Engineering's almost a trade but architecture's a *profession*."

I twist my hair around my finger and study it. The chlorine's turned it faintly green despite the special swimmer's shampoo I use.

"I don't care what she takes as long as she gets into a decent university," my mother says. "You are *world* class, Clarey, remember that."

"Well, what if I don't do either?" I hear my voice coming out of my mouth and it sounds like someone else's.

"What do you mean?" my father says. "Not medicine *or* law?"

Leonard and I escape to the Wasteland after dinner. It's the last week in July. The blue flax and the wild roses and vetch are done blooming and now it's more gaillardia, and yarrow. We start walking west down the chain link fence that divides the field from the trailer park. I take a trail to the right that heads down a bluff to the field closer to the highway. As we're trudging west up the dirt track where it curves up again, Leonard starts skittering around making sudden dashes away from me—and then he hides behind my leg and barks. He does this three times. I scan the bushes and tall grass to figure out why he's freaking out. Then I see her, just her mask, the buff colored snout and big alert ears, the yellow eyes beautifully outlined in black. She's crouched, peering down at the very edge of the slope above us, the setting sun outlining her fur from behind. Then she starts to do this slinky stalk through the scrub coming slowly down the bank towards us.

"Holy shit!" I breathe and feel for Leonard's collar. My arm flails around. Of course, no Leonard, who's dancing around like an idiot, and the coyote keeps slowly descending. *Don't freak*, I tell myself. A coyote won't attack a dog with its owner right there. I stand up as tall as I can and hold my hoodie out to each side to make myself look bigger. I stomp the ground and pretend to go at her.

"Hey!" I shout making my voice as deep as I can. "You get away, you big old gal coyote! We don't want to play with you. HEY! You get away!"

Leonard is making nervous Chihuahua yelps that don't exactly help, but she stops stalking and heads back up the bluff. I let out my breath and feel the adrenalin buzzing through me, but we're not done.

At the crest of the hill she turns and in the light of the

setting sun puffs herself up in all her grandeur. Then she starts to yip and yowl, and doesn't Leonard start talking back? I can't take me eyes off her as I lunge for his collar again. She does a chittery series of yips, looks at Leonard with her pretty eyes over her fluffy illuminated shoulder, and he takes off after her up the hill.

"Leonard you *idiot*!" I shout. I can't follow him up the bank. It's all wild rose scrub and I'm just wearing flip-flops. They disappear over the crest. I run as fast as I can up the dusty road yelling his name all the way. At the top of the hill I see the coyote loping full out, Leonard behind and gaining. They run towards the slough to the east.

"God damn it, LEONARD!" I shout, and then coming down the road from the west I see Jesus on his bike, his hair flying behind him in the wind. I keep running as hard as I can.

"I'll chase her off," he shouts, turning hard off the trail. He bounces over the rough ground and veers up the far side of the pond. The coyote and Leonard run full out up the near side. By now I'm standing on the bank and calculating the angles. If I swim straight across, I can intercept them before Jesus can reach them on his bike.

I tear off my purse and hoodie, kick off my flip-flops, and crouch. Take your mark. I rock back ten degrees and tighten every muscle. The pistol cracks and I explode, kicking as hard as I can with my right leg, my toes digging into the mud. I snap tight into a perfect streamline and fly airborne over the cattails and dimpled luminous water. The cold and gush and wash of the entry, the glide, and I'm cutting through the muddy water and the duckweed at a speed surpassing any personal best. In twenty strokes I reach the other bank, stagger out and fall on top of Leonard just as he dashes past. We're lying there panting, Leonard giving off whimpers of love for the vanishing coyote, and then Jesus's bike screeches and skids sideways beside us.

Making sure I've got a good grip on Leonard's collar, I roll over and look up at him.

"Fucking dog," I say. He stares at me, his lined brown face with the hair hanging down. Then he says slowly, he always does talk slowly:

"You sure are a brave one ... But I wouldn't do that again ... Don't be throwing yourself into that junk-filled slough for some silly dog! Don't know what's in there. I think there's an old car and lots of broken bottles ..." He trails off. "Good swimmer, too."

By the time I fill out just the basic information for Harvard, my eye twitches and my head hurts. The application packages for Yale and Brandeis are even longer. I have to get a SAT reasoning test done, and two SAT subject tests. I need two teacher evaluation forms filled in, I need to submit supplemental material demonstrating any 'exceptional talents,' the swimming, I guess. For Harvard last year, out of 34,303 applicants only 2,076 students made it in.

I've worked all afternoon, the west light sliding now across the thick white pile of my bedroom carpet. My parents are out for dinner with the Barrys again. From under all the others I pull out the slim U.B.C. application package in its manila envelope. I stare at it and then slide it back into hiding.

In the kitchen I lean against the cold marble counter and eat leftover veal meatloaf and saffron rice. In two more weeks, school starts back. Swim meets, and training camps consumed the whole summer except for the two weeks with my aunts and the cousins in Muskoka. It's only one more week till the big swim off. If I make the team and if my times are strong enough, I'll be 'carded' by the government. That's when we'll know if all the money, the endless driving and waiting and cheering, my parents' investment since I was ten, finally pays off. I get Leonard into the older Audi and we drive up to the Wasteland.

It's almost September. The sun illuminates the yellowing grasses, the rose bushes turn to russet. I breathe in the sage scented air and lift my eyes to a big poplar. It looks like an old galleon in the wind. Towering whipped-cream thunderheads pile up to the north. I try to visualize the race as I walk. There are people in the distance with their dogs. I do the bottom loop around the slough, and then I do the top loop in the west field. It is cooling off, but I don't want to go home. I pull the thick cuffs of my hoodie over my hands, put up the hood and zip it to my chin, and then I do another loop around the west field.

By the time I am on the straightaway back to my car, the wind whips my yoga pants around my legs and my ankles freeze above my runners. I hold onto my hood, and then it starts to rain. It doesn't ease into it, just starts pelting me at a forty-five-degree angle. In a minute the left side of my body is drenched. I look up and see someone through the rain, wrestling a carpet off the chain link fence and bundling it onto the back porch of a trailer. The rain turns to hail, first the size of peas, then the size of shooter marbles, and it stings when it hits like some sort of barbaric massage at my mother's spa. The person dragging in the carpet runs back out through the gate in the fence, and shouts to me, but I can't hear. When I get close, whoever it is takes my arm and turns me. I look up from beneath the dripping hood hanging over my face and realize it's Jesus.

"You'd better wait it out," he yells. "It's gonna be a bad one." Leonard, of course, dashes into the yard past the meat stump and onto a covered porch attached to the short end of the trailer. Jesus opens a door at the side of the trailer and waits for me to go in. The hail pounds down harder now. One like a ping-pong ball smashes into my temple and makes my head spin. Leonard makes a dash from the porch to the side door, so there's nothing else to do. I cross the yard and just walk in. I push back my hood and stand there shaking and dripping on a threadbare doormat. When I blink the rain out of my eyelashes, the doormat reads Home Sweet Home. The dogs all start barking

"We've got a visitor, babe," Jesus says when the dogs calm down. "This one's pretty brave, but I think she'd better wait it out." A woman with long grey hair sits watching a documentary on aliens and crop circles, crocheting one of those Barbie doll ballerina toilet roll covers. My second cousin's mother had one centered on her toilet tank. Cecile said it was too tacky for words, but I kind of wanted a matching one. The woman, babe, is tanned and lean and I can't tell how old she is either.

"You're soaked!" she says. "Just a minute." And goes into a back room.

"I'm going to go change," Jesus says. I stand there dripping with my teeth knocking together. In a minute babe comes back and hands me a faded leopard print towel. I take it and rub my hair dry. Then she wraps a polyester pile blanket with two black lab puppies on it around my shoulders. It smells clean and feels really warm.

"Thank you," I say.

"Sit here." She smiles and motions to a bar stool beside the kitchen counter. "I'll make you hot chocolate. So, you're the coyote gal Rob's been talking about."

"I thought that was almost the end of my dumb dog! If that coyote ate Leonard, my parents would have flipped out!" I don't mention they think I shouldn't walk up here. I don't want to be rude.

"Well, you know what they say about Coyote, don't you?"

"No. What?"

"The Navajo called Coyote 'the shape shifter.' When Coyote shows up expect a change, an ending. But that always means a new beginning too. Coyote accompanied the first man and woman into their new life."

"When one door closes another door opens?" I say, playing along. I notice all the crystals hanging from threads in the little slider kitchen window. An abundant spider plant hangs over the sink in a macramé hanger.

"Yes, like that."

Babe boils the kettle and spoons Carnation hot chocolate mix out of a jar into mismatched coffee mugs. My mother makes hot chocolate with Dutch process cocoa, William and Sonoma vanilla paste, and organic whole milk.

Jesus comes out of the bedroom dressed in sweat pants and an old t-shirt.

"Let's go sit on the back porch and watch the storm," he says. "That's the main reason I built it."

He opens the door at the end of the living room and we all step out with our mugs and the dogs. We sit down on an orange plaid sofa. I sit at the far end, then Babe, then Jesus. The springs are blown in the seat, and it sucks me down so I'm not sure I can get out without someone hauling me up. But the suctioning sofa makes me feel kind of cocooned, and I snuggle down into the blanket and wrap my hands around my mug. I think of my parents' down filled natural suede sofas from Montauk. You can't sit on them in wet pants.

We stare out at the scrubland, at the shifting sheets of hail and rain, at the trees bending and lashing in the wind. Jesus puts his arm around Babe and kisses her on her shiny grey hair. He looks down the couch at me and lifts his mug.

"Doesn't get better than this," he yells, and I lift my mug back at him.

Nothing more needs to be said, and we couldn't say it anyhow, over the din. We sit there for probably fifteen minutes. I feel the knots in my stomach and shoulders relax. I realize, after a while, that my eyebrow isn't even twitching. The disciples and Leonard all line up along the edge of the porch staring into the rain. I drink my cocoa. It is too sweet and watery, with a chemical finish, but the heat of it warms me from the roof of my mouth to the bottom of my stomach, and it tastes somehow of freedom.

When the storm is over, I thank them, and have to give them back the black lab puppy blanket.

"I'm sorry," I say. "I got it all wet. Thank you so much! You've been so kind. Thank you for the cocoa and keeping me from getting hailed to death!" Babe and Jesus look at me calmly.

"No worries," Jesus says.

"Better get home before it's dark," babe says. She turns to him. "The coyote might be out now that the storm's over, hey? Maybe you'd better follow her on the bike just to be sure."

"I'll go get my bike out," Jesus says. "You get a head start on us, but I'll be around. I want to check out the damage."

I wave to the two of them on the porch. Then I latch the gate in the chain link fence behind me, and Leonard and I take off running like crazy, through the sideways light catching in the millions of raindrops clinging to branches. As I run, I see myself, the perfect racing dive into the slough, the cattails, the murk, the mud between my toes as they leave the ground, and Jesus saying: "Don't throw yourself into that junk filled slough for a silly dog! Who knows what's in there." And the green smell of chlorophyll from the hail mashed plants rises up around Leonard and me. It rises up in cool waves, and we run.

Intersection

Saturday morning Julie pulls the dark red sweater over her head, the same red as the frozen crabapples knocking on the window in the wind. Just a visit to their old house, one last visit, and her stomach twists tighter. A masochistic exercise really. To run her hand down the handrails, stand in their attic bedroom and smell the remnants of their life there. Lou rents a condo in Rundle now. In three days, the realtor will rekey the locks, her and Lou's keys obsolete, and the new owners will move in. Food seems impossible, so she makes coffee while her cat scrapes his whiskered jowls against her shins.

She studies this rented kitchen, the yellowing checkerboard linoleum, the old wooden cabinets. It should be charming if it wasn't so dysfunctional. Lou gave her the French press coffee pot and it's the only thing that looks like home. Julie suddenly feels again his heat, the solidity against her back, his hand on her sternum between her breasts. She turns and presses her forehead against the upper cabinet, the too short counter cutting her hips, and kicks the lower door. It bounces. Fucking thing never would latch.

Dave's eyes open and settle on the satin freckled skin between Chloe's shoulder blades. He remembers loving Saturday mornings. Saturdays, when they were lucky to make it to brunch at Dairy Lane by noon. He runs his hand tentatively along the smooth slope of her hip. No response. Very gently, he strokes her stomach, the line of downy fuzz that runs below her belly button.

"Ummh," she says and stirs in her sleep. Hopefully his hand travels up to explore her daily more turgid breasts, the nipples now like small marshmallows, tender and puffy.

"Don't," she says, flinging his hand off and rolling face down.

"I'm sleeping," she mumbles from behind the tangle of red gold silk, her face thrust into the pillow.

He lies on his back and stares at the ceiling. Another Saturday morning taking care of things in the shower by himself. To hell with this. He lies there for five minutes and listens to her breath getting deep and regular again. Well, he'd go to hot yoga, that's what he'd do. He still went once a month. Initially he'd bought a membership to impress Chloe. The studio proved as torpid as a jungle, in the dim light incandescent sweating women in impossible poses reflected back in the wall of mirrors. You could watch everything and never even turn your head.

He dresses, pulling sweat pants over running shorts, a t-shirt and a hoodie. As he brushes his teeth and hair, he decides his day-old stubble looks Saturday appropriate, and slips off his wedding ring. He places it in the cabinet beside the dental floss; he almost lost it once when it slid of his sweat slick finger in the middle of class. In the kitchen he eats a power bar and fills his water bottle at the sink.

He wonders if she'll be there again, with her dark eyes and Ani DiFranco vibe. After class she'd sat on the bench in the lobby beside him, lacing up her boots, and he felt this intimacy after ninety minutes side-by-side, stretching and bending and practically naked.

"The ride's gonna be refreshing," he said, gesturing with a rueful grin towards the window, the snow ratcheting sideways, whipped to a frenzy by the descending north front.

She looked up, brushing long strands of hair from her eyes.

"You even ride your bike in the winter? I should do that, I feel so guilty about my car. It's such a gas guzzler."

"Yup, I've got a mountain bike with really knobby tires. It's just a little way I can do my part." He watched her face open and her blue eyes dilate as she smiled up at him.

"I ride in the summer, but I worry about the ice. I'll bring my bike into the shop and get some proper tires! There, you just inspired me!"

"As long as I wear the right gear, I'm actually really comfortable all winter" he said. "Well, have a good day!"

He smiled back and could feel her watching him as went out the door. He loitered around the bike rack messing with his gym bag and someone else's bike. She passed him with another smile, and when she was out of sight, he turned the corner down the side street and hopped into his frozen Jeep. It was so easy. You just figured out what they cared about, and then you gave it to them.

This morning he laces up his runners and opens the

kitchen door. No need for a note. He'll be back before Chloe wakes up.

The recently purchased pale grey Fiat 500 looks like a kid's toy in the snow. They decided Lou should keep the Ford Focus. Julie hacks at the ice spackled windscreen till she chips a circle clear on the driver's side. She gets in and starts it up, turns the vents to high, then goes and works on the other windows. Every morning before he went to work Lou had done this for her, got her car heated up, brushed off the snow. Julie gets back in and sits there waiting for the windshield to defrost. She makes herself think about the puppy.

No, first had been the station wagon. Their old Toyota Celica blew a valve, and the oil haemorrhaged onto the street. She had started it without realizing and totalled the engine. They rented a car since it was a Monday and planned on going car shopping on the weekend. But on Wednesday he got out of work early and showed up that night with a moss green Ford Focus.

"It's practically a minivan. Why do we need something this big?"

"No, it's not. Just a roomy station wagon. It'll be good for hauling stuff for the garden."

"You should have called me and asked! I mean, I just can't see myself driving around in a minivan *or* a station wagon for that matter!" She sat in the front seat with the window rolled down on one of those last mellow October days.

"Well, I think it looks good on you," he said from the sidewalk. "You look sexy in a stations wagon *or* a minivan. I wanted to surprise you. It was a great deal."

She acquiesced. It proved an easier car for the canoe and camping gear. She remembers those trips, the two of them paddling through teal beaver flats, the quiet, his presence, the jokes. Sitting beside riverbanks while he fished, and she worked out another article on her laptop.

On weekends like today he cooked. He loved it actually; it decompressed him after work. It used to make her feel guilty till she realized he wanted to. Lamb with garlic and rosemary slow roasting while they went for a ride on the bikes. He'd gone through a long Moroccan phase, making his own preserved lemons, slicing them and layering them with coarse salt in a mason jar. In a month they jammified into amber, to use in his chicken and olive tagines. By this time on a Saturday morning, he'd have started the weekly batch of wholegrain bread to rise, filling the house with its yeasty breath. Did he still do that, alone in the rented condo?

She makes herself remember the puppy.

On her 32nd birthday. Lou came into the bedroom with a vibrating and bumping cardboard box, tied with a big red ribbon.

"What on earth ..." The box whined and released a stream of warm liquid over her knee. She pulled off the ribbon and opened the flaps. A wriggling Springer Spaniel puppy scratched at her chest, licked her neck and bit her chin.

"Good God," Julie said.

"I'll just leave you two alone to get acquainted. You're going to love him! Happy birthday darling." And he dashed off to work so fast he forgot to give her a kiss.

There was no way to get anything written that day, and she needed to email the article to *Alberta Review* by the afternoon. If the dog wasn't shitting on the carpet, he was chewing up their chess set. She'd been foolish enough to think a blissful quiet spell meant he was sleeping, while he gnawed efficiently through the left partner of her prized black boots. If she put him in the crate that Lou left in the kitchen, he howled. The only way to keep him still was to hold him on her lap with one hand while she typed with the other. Thus stupefied by her body heat, he eventually fell asleep. The minute she laid him on the carpet though, he woke up and the dance started again.

When Lou came home, she met him at the back door and handed him the puppy.

"I can't," she said.

The red jeep warms up as Dave plays with the channels on the radio. Chloe kept setting it to soft rock, but today he felt like something high school, greatest hits of the '80s. Giving up on the radio, he finds his favourite Van Halen CD in the glove compartment. This early on a Saturday morning the streets are deserted. Only the occasional geriatric insomniac shovels a walk, but everyone else is in bed. An uninviting icy day, but he feels about sixteen as he drives the jeep into the parking lot beside the rec centre. He jacks it sideways, so snow flies up beside him. He pulls a few donuts to "You Really Got Me," bellowing and pounding on the steering wheel. The clock in the dash reads eight thirty. He needs get to the studio in the next ten minutes if he wants to find a spot to lay his mat.

He takes Sixth Avenue for ten blocks, driving twenty kilometres over the speed limit. "I've got it *BAD, SO BAD, I'm hot for teacher.*" The sun finds a crack beneath the grey ceiling and bursts out sideways. Glancing up empty Fourteenth Street, he whips into the intersection, the Jeep fishtailing wildly and he's about to shout for the sheer joy of propulsion, when a horn honks like the bleat of a goat. In his rear-view mirror he sees a small grey car spin and skid sideways, receding in the sparkling glare of snow crystals and the icy street in the sun. Everything goes into slow mo. Dave watches transfixed as the tiny car slides, hopelessly, inevitably sideways and then with a resounding crunch melds itself onto a red Canada Post mailbox. The car and the mailbox married now, as the Fiat's passenger side wraps around it in a permanent steely embrace. He winces at the whiplash no doubt recoiling inside the little car.

"Oh shit!" Dave says. "Shit, shit, shit!!"

Julie took Kensington Road west. *A baby*, she thought. She'd held one two nights ago at her old friend Lola's house. She'd held it with her arms straight out, the baby dangling in the air with an alarmed look on its face.

"No, no. Like this silly. Sit here on the couch." Lola shoved a pillow under her arm. "Now put his head in the crook of your elbow, and the other arm wraps around him like that so he feels nice and snug. There you go." He looked up at her, his tiny old man face grimacing magenta, and grunted.

"Is he going to cry? What's he doing?"

Lola laughed. "Oh, he's *very* comfortable with you, I think he's pooping!"

"Oh! Goodness." The odd yogurt reek percolated suddenly from the tenuous containment of the washable diaper.

"Here give him to me. I'll go change him." Julie followed Lola into the bedroom. On a towel laid on the bed, she stripped the terry cloth sleeper off his legs, tucking them up behind his shoulders, then she peeled open the Velcro tabs.

"Quick, could you throw me that washcloth?" Julie tossed it to her as Lola opened the diaper, and with some maternal lightning sleight of hand covered his miniscule penis. "You've got to be quick. Twice he got me in the eye."

"With what?"

"Pee, silly! It seems to be some sort of reflex to cold air, I don't know. But it happens every time!" With his wrinkled feet in one hand, she pulled up on his bandy legs and lifted his hips. His creased little butt covered with what looked like seedy Dijon mustard.

"When they're breastfeeding their poop's not too toxic. How you doing, buddy?" she crooned. The baby smiled drunkenly, his eyes not quite synchronized. She swabbed his buttocks and scrotum clean with a wet wipe, slathered everything with a white sticky paste, and then strapped him into a clean diaper.

"How often do you have to *do* that?'

"Oh, I don't know, maybe seven times a day? I change him right away. I wouldn't want my wittle mankin to get a diaper rash, would I, buddy? I've got to feed him now. Come on, let's go back to the living room." On the couch again, Lola pulled out her breast, and Julie watched transfixed as her friend's nipple suddenly elongated into a half-inch tube, spraying milk like a sprinkler. "Quick! Get on there, buddy, ah, there you go." The baby snorfled into her breast. His hands pressed and released alternately against her chest as if trying to pump the milk out of her even faster. Julie took a deep breath.

"How often do you do *that*?"

"Oh God, he's going through a growth spurt right now, so I really don't know. Fifteen times maybe, and three times in the night."

"Jesus!"

"Yeah. I know. It's the weirdest thing. I went through thirty-two hours of labour. They eventually had to induce me and pull him out with forceps, and I am *not* kidding you, the doctor had his foot up on the table. Add that to ten months of pregnancy. I just remember thinking: 'This is the most outrageously difficult thing I have ever done, this *can't* be worth it.'" Lola smiled at her from the corner of the couch and Julie stared back at her once so hip friend, now with the dark circles under her eyes and the extra twenty pounds of 'baby weight.'

"But you know, I still can't get over this. When they laid him on my chest, and he looked at me, it was crazy because it *was*."

"Was what?"

"Worth it! Actually, I've never done anything more worthwhile in my entire life." She put the baby up on her shoulder and started to pat his back.

"Uuurp," he said, spitting curdled milk over her shirt and hitting the couch in the bargain.

Julie went home and washed the new puppy smell off in the shower and put her clothes immediately in the machine. She knew the smell of twenty-years' hard labour.

Now driving back to their house for one last look, she remembers Lou at parties, how she'd be upstairs talking shop and he'd vanish, and she'd finally find him in the rumpus room rolling around on the rug with any available kids. One night in particular she caught him riding a trike, his knees almost hitting his chin as he chased a little girl shrieking around the basement. The poor bastard, he just couldn't help it.

Julie turns right off Kensington onto deserted Fourteenth Street. At the door Lola said: "I was never into babies before, but he's *my* baby, you know?"

No. No, I don't know, Julie thought. *And I can't.*

At Sixth Street, she'd turn left and drive past their house. If the station wagon was parked in front, she'd just keep going. Her hand goes up for the turn signal. In her peripheral vision she sees something red flying at her, and she jerks the steering wheel to the right. On the slick road the Fiat spins in a circle and then slides sideways as she slams her foot uselessly and repeatedly on the brake. Her head snaps back, and her ears pop with the detonation of steel on steel as the passenger side of the car smashes into a red mailbox on the corner.

The car ticks and gurgles. Her neck hurts and her head swims. She tries to figure out the mess of trajectory trailing behind this moment. She searches the control panel for the emergency light button but she can't find it. The car is so new to her and she'd only skimmed the manual. Her hands shake as she flips through the book trying to find the index. Nothing makes sense, and then, with the same brain stem pivot and swerve with which she'd missed the Jeep, her hand takes the phone from the console. Lou. Dial.

Well, he hadn't actually hit her. For a moment his foot hovers over the gas pedal, but then he pulls over and parks kitty corner to the mailbox. He digs through the glove compartment and finds the plastic envelope with the pink insurance slip. He gets a pen and a Dunkin Donuts napkin off the floor to write on, climbs out of the jeep and walks back to the little mangled car. The young woman rolls down the window and looks up at him, her grey eyes astonished. She talks into a cell phone.

"My car! I mean ... I've hit a mailbox and I think it's totalled! I'm fine. It's just my car, and I'm on Fourteenth Street ... Someone almost hit me ... Ok ... in a minute ... Ok."

Her hand with the phone sinks to her lap and she looks up at Dave. Her shell-shocked face reminds him of Chloe two months ago when she came out of the bathroom after peeing on the stick.

"Shit! I'm *so* sorry! Are you okay? I didn't see you. I guess that's obvious. I think we call the police at this point. Are you okay?"

"Uh, yeah. I think so. But my car! I bought it two weeks ago. I can't believe this. I didn't see you coming! Do you have the, um, what do you call it? I need your insurance. Lou says I need your insurance."

On the way home Dave stops at the Seven Eleven and buys a litre of milk for their coffee. He comes into the kitchen, then stops. Retching sounds from the bathroom again. He finds Chloe kneeling over the toilet in her pyjamas, her knuckles white, hanging on to the sides. The strawberry blond gloss of hair falls forward into the line of fire. Dave steps up and does his best to hold it out of the way. She convulses again and rests. One more time.

Dave takes a towel from the rack and wets it with cold water. He wrings it out and waits. Now she's only dry heaving. Yes, she's finished. When Chloe stands, he holds the back of her head to keep her steady, and with the towel he wipes her down: the sweat off her forehead, the salty slick from under her bloodshot eyes, the vomit off of her chin. He goes to the kitchen and grabs a glass, comes back and fills it from the tap.

"Here," he says, handing it to her. "Rinse and spit."

Shelterbelt

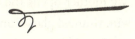

A family lived in our house in the 1940s. Not the people who built it, I think, but the family after. Late one winter, the river rose with the spring thaw and flooded our street. The water filled the basements and then the first stories. This was before they'd built the Bearspaw Dam to stop the ice jam flooding. The family couldn't leave by the road and maybe they ran out of food, because they decided to hike out on the railway tracks. They made it to main street Bowness and the grocery store, but as they walked their feet froze in their soaking boots. Later their toes fell off. I lie in bed and I listen to the train coming. The tracks run past the back of our lot, and I imagine that toeless family. Were they like Weebles after that, tilting and rocking on their useless feet?

Our house sits on almost an acre. Along the chain-link fence that separates us from the CP land, poplars grow parallel with the tracks the full length of our dead-end road. When I was twelve and we moved here, I woke up every time the train went by. Now I don't even hear it. Sometimes I'm eating dinner or doing homework and I look up and notice the wavy panes in the old sash windows vibrating. And only after that do I hear the train.

My mother opens the door, dressed for work, her round wire rimmed glasses and hippy hair in its ponytail.

"You'd better get going, honey. You slept in." I look at the clock and it says 7:15. Half an hour to get breakfast and dress, if I jump the tracks instead of going the long way round, I can make it to Social Studies by eight. I pull on my not tight enough jeans, my halter style bra with its two triangles of insufficiently nipple concealing nylon, a t-shirt that should reference a rock band but doesn't, and a grey hoodie. I brush out the hair that falls to the middle of my back. I try to make my bangs "feather," sweep out like wings along my temples. But my mother still cuts my hair and they migrate back to a straight line across my forehead no matter how much mousse I use.

My dad and sister have already left. My mother shouts goodbye on her way out the door. The VW Rabbit backs down the driveway. I tie up my runners and put on the rated to minus forty Michelin Man coat my dad insists I wear. At least I can hide my toque and gloves in my pocket on the last block to school.

It's the beginning of April, and a wet dump of snow came down last night. Our road, Bow Crescent, threading between the river and the railway track, is like a country lane in the city. They even forgot to put in sidewalks. I follow in a tire rut to keep the snow out of my shoes, anything but wearing my monster Sorrels. At the dead end I hit the CPR chain link fence. Concealed behind the board fence of Shannon Burke's house is a narrow passage just a foot of space, and here my sister and Russell Dobson cut the chain link with my father's wire clippers. I'm about to slide through when I realize they've sewn it tight shut with heavy gauge wire. The CPR is getting quicker. This time they found our hole in under a month. I kick the fence.

"Fuck!"

Further down in view of the street is the other option, a two-foot section where the jabbing top wires of the chain link are bent over from all the kids climbing. I grab a hold of the top rail here and ram my toe into the chain link as high as I can. I pull myself up and my other foot goes to the top rail. For a moment I balance on just my hand and foot and then I jump down into CP land. I can see where Dwight and Angus walked ahead of me. I follow their footsteps up the rise onto the train tracks. Southeast, the poplars run parallel with the tracks in their lacey interlapping beauty. West, the rusted trestles sit brooding in the sun waiting for the next Vancouver bound train. I stay here as long as I can in CP land, the space between home and school. But I'll be late, so I hurry and jump the other fence, and then as usual I pick up Josh's footsteps. He lives further south, on the other side of the tracks. But my back yard and his front yard almost exactly line up. I can see the lights of his upstairs bedroom through the trees when I'm lying in bed.

Two blocks and up a hill, and there looms the brick monolith of Bowness High. The bell has just rung and the crowds funnel in. Cigarette butts litter the snow on the front lawn. I follow the sidewalk mottled with black gum and fossilized spit and cross the threshold.

Marcie Phelps pushes past me, almost knocking my backpack off my shoulder. Her eyes scrape past me and keep going. She wears a tiny hot pink and grey, hip-grazing ski jacket. She sees her friend Crystal Malloy and they start laughing about some party they went to on the weekend. Their hair brushes their shoulders and feathers back in perfect wings. I head up the stairwell. The second-floor sports ancient beige linoleum, with orange and black streaks. Battleship grey lockers crowd shoulder to shoulder down the length of the hall. In the hubbub I spin my lock, put my pack away and pull out my social studies binder. Someone touches my shoulder.

"Hey Zoe." There stand Angus and Dwight.

"Hi guys."

"First meeting for the Yearbook Club tonight. Just wanted to be sure you could make it. Three-thirty in the social studies open area." Angus with his beseeching smile.

Across the hall I see Josh hanging up his coat in his locker. My palms start to sweat. I cringe a little for him to see me with Dwight and Angus, but it's not as if I have any social standing to speak of anyhow.

"Uh, yeah guys, I'll be there."

Next time I glance up Marcie Phelps has snuggled up to Josh. He smiles down at her, leans in, and with one hand he brushes the hair off her cheek. His other hand balances his binder against his muscular thigh.

In Social Studies Mr. Pfeifer tries to get the class to concentrate on the political climate in pre-Nazi-Germany. The guys fall out of their chairs and sit backwards and snigger. Mr. Pfeifer snaps chalk into pieces behind his back, and then whips one across the room nailing Daryl Crain in the side of the head. The whole class laughs.

"Hey, that's abuse!" Daryl says to Glenn Dronsfield, rubbing his temple, but he seems kind of pleased. The noise level in the classroom doesn't falter. I think about the rest of the morning. After this I have math and then Phys. Ed. My palms *and* my armpits start to sweat. Volleyball. Last class I almost sprained a finger and eyes roll when my name gets called for a team. I think I'll skip out after math class. I'm on the honour roll. I can get away with it now and then. Outside the sun liberates mushy clots of snow that fall from the roof past the windows.

I look into my father's study on the way to my room. Coffee cups and wine glasses are strewn everywhere. Once a month my sister or I go up there with a box and take them all back to the kitchen. Islands of mould float in puddles of black coffee. This Saturday morning my father lies on a beach towel on the carpet, a pillow under his head. He wears black Spandex bike shorts pulled over his bulging stomach. Round black rubber pads stick to each of his major muscle groups. I know he dipped them in soapy water to help them achieve a good seal through all the hair. A wire runs from each rubber pad back to the control box. Through his massive earphones I hear the Mozart blasting. Muscles twitch in unison all over his body under the rubber disks. His eyes open and he pulls the earphones to one side.

"Zoe, could you turn up the voltage two notches?" I step over his legs and turn the dial. The peculiar musk of my father permeates the room he practically lives in. I watch his muscles all jump in unison. He replaces the earphones and closes his eyes.

In my bedroom, I shut the door. The long south window has a view of the poplars running parallel with the track. Through it I can just make out Josh Leighton's house on the far side of the shelterbelt and CP land. In the winter it's better, without any leaves. I wonder what he's doing over there, maybe shooting hoops in the driveway, or practicing his holds on his family's basement climbing wall. Josh's family is seriously into mountaineering.

I sit down at my desk in front of the long window and pull out my watercolour paper, bamboo brushes and pencils. I start on a mixed media drawing of the poplars for my art class. I want to capture their generosity and optimism. Somehow catch their dance with the wind, the sap waking up inside of them, and the thousands of pieces of sky held between the branches. I start with my HB pencil.

Kelly's mum Margaret is British, though actually Kelly says she was born in Canada. She only lived in London when she was a teenager and a young woman after the war, but her Cockney accent is as fresh as if she just stepped off the plane from London. If you get her talking about the Queen, she starts to cry. It's one in the afternoon on Sunday and I ride my yellow ten-speed up the crescent to Kelly's house. Kelly is really my sister Lindsay's friend. I know they're already there, probably hanging out in Kelly's room talking about horses and boys. They've never kicked me out, at least not yet. I weave around puddles of melted snow, letting go of the handlebars and see how far I can get just steering with my hips like Josh. Bam, immediately I hit a pothole and almost go over the top.

When I get to Kelly's house, I lean my bike against the wall of their garage, leave my shoes on the doormat and open the door.

"Hello," I call.

"Hi pet." Margaret smiles at me from the kitchen. She wears a silky purple blouse, three buttons undone. It's belted with a wide red sash, accentuating her waist and curvaceous hips in their tight black capris. She stands at the kitchen sink smoking and looking at the river. Her auburn hair is lustrous in its asymmetrical layered waves. In the study off the kitchen I see Kelly's dad sitting in his recliner, watching hockey as usual. His hand holds a stubby glass of whiskey on the armrest. He doesn't hear me or turn around. I try to remember the last time I actually saw his face.

"Come over here and see these cheeky bastards, Zoe," Margaret says. I walk over and look through the window at three magpies in the snow. Two are locked in battle, a tug of war over a twig, one leans back so far, his tail bends backwards mashed into the snow. We laugh.

"They must be nest building."

"Remember this, Zoe. It's the *little* things, the *little* things that keep you going, like these cheeky buggers. Bits of joy. You have to collect them." Her eyes wander out onto the river, the ice breaking up in the thaw, and under the foundation her face looks old. She turns to me.

"Luv, you're so pretty." She runs her fingers through my hair letting it fall as it always does, straight in front of my shoulders. She tugs at my grey hoodie. "Someone's got to help you out." She leans towards me and I can smell her perfume, I think Charlie or maybe Obsession? "Would your mum mind if I gave you a little haircut?"

After math I go stash my binder. I loiter around my locker waiting till everyone's gone to their next class, then bunch my Michelin Man coat under my arm as small as possible and walk past the classrooms full of scraping chairs and teachers' voices. I slip down two flights of stairs, past the wall of Bowness Graduates, 1964 all the way to 1983, and the guidance counsellor's office whose door is luckily closed. Through the vestibule and I am free. I breathe in the sharp air. My dad will be home because he doesn't have to teach till the afternoon. I can hang out on CP land and then show up at lunchtime.

I jump the fence and cross the track, and then turn east away from the river, down the gravel road that the CP guys use for maintenance work. The snow is no match for the spring sun. I hear a woodpecker ratatat-tatting and snow falling off trees in soft plops. A wind picks up and the poplars bend and sway, a momentary snowstorm blows sideways off the trees. The ice crystals catch in the light and melt on my cheek. Then the wind dies, and all is quiet again. For a minute I walk eyes closed, moving through pockets of cold snowmelt air, and then pockets of sun warmed stillness. The organic funk of defrosting leaf mould rises rich and earthy. A cacophony of geese erupts. I open my eyes as they fly above in V formation, following the tracks like a runway and headed for a river landing.

I walk till I come to the back of our property. Most of the poplars lie on the residential side of the fence, but a few grow in CP land. I've reached my destination, an old poplar that splits into two trunks six feet up. It's dying out in its crown and riddled with woodpecker holes. I get my foot up to a broken branch and scramble to the cleft, then higher onto a dip in one of the sloping trunks. I can see my dad's car still parked behind the house. He'll leave soon and then I'll go home. From here I can see perfectly into Josh's front yard. The Volvo is parked in front, so his mom must be home. She has black hair and blue blue eyes, just like Josh. I saw her one day when I walked past in the fall, bringing Kentucky Fried Chicken in from the car. I don't think my mother has ever even stepped inside one of the Colonel's restaurants.

I look up at the branch tips of my tree. Their grey knuckled joints and the sharp brown buds straining upwards. Multitudes of them all waiting to erupt when Mother Nature whistles. A pair of harried chickadees flit with grass and twigs, stuffing them into an abandoned woodpecker hole, on their urgent mission to proliferate. My Michelin Man coat provides ample padding against the rough bark of the poplar. I brace my feet against two branches, lean back in the sun, and watch them as they work.

In Margaret's kitchen Kelly and my sister stand back, heads tilted and hands on hips as they squint at me balanced on a kitchen stool. The scissors shear off ten-inch locks of hair with a rasping "schick." They fall like feathers against my arms and collect in a blond cloud on my lap.

"This is the important bit," Margaret says. She parts my China chop bangs in the middle, combs them, fanning them out against my cheek. I feel the cool steel of the scissors touch my face, angling up towards my nose from the jawline. Schick, schick. Now the other side.

"Wow, that looks great, Mum!"

Lindsay laughs. "Hey, little sister?"

"I'll just layer and texturize a bit," Margaret says.

In English class we read for the last half hour. I open my book, *One Day in the Life of Ivan Denisovich*. In minutes I am lost in the gulag: how a successful day means a bit of fat in some soup, how a favour exchanged might bring a less threadbare blanket, how something so tiny can equal hope. I look up at the students around me. I want to shout, to say: "Oh my God, can you imagine? This is amazing! You've got to read this!" But I hold it in hard and keep my face blank. To reveal actual interest spells social catastrophe. I could tell Angus but then he'd be on me again to play *Dungeons and Dragons* with the debate team. The final bell rings. We scramble our books together and burst out of the door into the hallway.

The senior basketball team practices Fridays after school. I might as well go hang out and watch. I sit at the very back of the bleachers by Renee Blackwater. Renee lives in subsidized housing on Bowness Road. We lean back against the Bowness Trojans insignia painted on the concrete block wall in gold and green. The loudspeakers blare "Heartache Tonight" and the senior guys in their green and gold gym strip move like a dance through a passing and dribbling drill. Josh waits his turn. The basketball, dribbling as sure and steady as a drumbeat, with each bounce leaps to his hand as if pulled by a string, kind of like my heart. I run my eyes over his chiselled jaw, the shiny black hair, his piercing blue eyes, how his back fills out his t-shirt.

"Josh is so hot," Renee says, breathing into my ear.

"Do you think?"

"Look over there." She gestures with her chin towards the gym door. Out in the hall I see Marcie Phelps sort of doubled over against the wall with her face in her hands. Crystal Malloy rubs her back and looks up and down the hall, then leans forward to talk to her. "They broke up, you know. I think he's going with Janice Curzon now."

"You think so? Really? Already?"

"Well, we'll know tomorrow if they're holding hands," Renee says. "Every girl in this school wants to date him. He can pick anyone he wants to."

I watch for half an hour, but I leave before practice ends. I don't want to walk home at the same time as Josh.

After I jump the fence, I stand for a minute on the high ground of the tracks. The sun warms my back. It's Friday and I don't have to go back for two days. I breathe in the wet sap sweetness of the poplar buds, the smoky choke of creosote from the railway ties, and realize I love both smells equally. Balancing on the burnished steel rail, I make my wavering way to the trestle. The length of my legs makes the trestle hard to walk. The ties are too close together for a regular step, but two of them are too far apart unless I stretch. I must mince or leap. This is because my legs are proportionally too short. I know because an article in *Mademoiselle* said they should be at least three inches longer than your torso. I measured mine and they are actually an inch shorter than my torso. So that makes me four inches inadequate. Today I mince, and the tourmaline water rushes underneath me doing funny things with my eyes. I have to keep refocusing on the ties and where to put my feet. The dyke of gravel in the middle of the river pulls me. It's where the twin trestles meet. If you stand on that dyke, you're too far from either bank to get across in time when a train comes. Lindsay says, if that happens, since there's no way to outrun it, you have to jump down onto the lower beam of the trestle, with nothing but air and the river below you and the train roaring above. She says Russell Dobson did it.

Kids dive off the very top of the trestles and swim over to the bank. Last summer I was way up the road in the park by Kelly's house, and I saw them pull a boy out of the river. I guess he'd belly flopped. He was grey blue. I lay with my stomach on the sun-warmed steel of the roundabout, and

I could hear his poor deluded mother talking to a policeman. She kept saying "when I get him home, he's going to *get it!*" all the while they were loading him onto a stretcher.

I walk till I'm only a quarter of the way out on the first trestle and sit on the end of a tie with my feet dangling over, my arm around the rusty steel upright beside me. I watch the water rushing green over submerged ice. I suddenly think what time it is, because there's Josh coming down the road from school, still in his gold and green Trojans' uniform. I pull back against the metal and watch him as he turns the corner for home, and luckily, he doesn't see me.

"What is this schlop?" my father asks, poking at the food on his plate.

"Walnut balls in an almond milk béchamel sauce. Very high in protein but totally meat free!" my mother says.

"What's wrong with a little meat? I'd just like a little meat now and then." His chair scrapes across the floor. "I have a headache, actually. I think I'll go take a nap." He stomps upstairs to his study and bangs the door.

My mother looks at me brightly and asks how my day went. "Remember the Krishnamurti meditation group comes over Sunday afternoon, so you'll need to get your cleaning done on Saturday. Lindsay, you have the living room this week, and Zoe's got bathrooms, right?"

Lindsay and I mumble into our walnut balls and brown rice.

"Oh, and Saturday at three is the appointment with the Iridologist. I want him to look at both you girls. He says you can diagnose so much about a person's health just by looking at their iris."

"What's wrong with my health?" Lindsay asks. "I'm perfectly healthy. I didn't even get a cold this winter."

"Well, if it weren't for Dr. Schuster I never would have known about the buildup in my descending colon and then I wouldn't have done the cleansing fast that cleared everything out. It's preventative. Let me look at your eyes again, Zoe." She turns my face into the sunshine. "See how it looks kind of lacey at around three o'clock in the right eye. That's the descending colon. That area should look clearer. I think you could be developing a buildup too."

In the art room Mr. Bailey stands at the sink working on a bucket of encrusted paint brushes that he left soaking for a week. He's not too good at housekeeping, I guess. This room is splattered and caked with paint. It smells of ink and clay. I come here whenever I can, during lunch or spares or after school. The muffled beat of Aerosmith filters down the hall from the gym.

"What are you doing here?" he asks. "You should be at the dance! Go have some fun."

I look down at my sneakers and try to sound nonchalant but come up with nothing but a muffled: "It's kind of loud." I will him not to kick me out. If I can get him talking, he'll go on for an hour at least. I think about which of his favourite topics to pick: how he used to box, his horses, or maybe printmaking in Alberta after the war. Finally, I just say: "Do you want me to do the brushes?"

"Well, I might as well put you to work if you're hanging around." He wipes his hands on a paint rag and moves over to let me into the sink. I dump out the murky water in the bucket, getting down to the soft sedimentary ooze at the bottom. Under the tap I rub the bristles of a brush into the palm of my hand till the water runs clear, scrape the leathery collar of paint off the metal neck with my fingernails, and put it upright to dry in the big pickle jar by the sink.

I realize he isn't going off on one of his diatribes like usual and look up to see him watching me.

"Your painting of the shelterbelt impressed me, Zoe," he says. "Actually, it made me really proud. There's something I thought you'd be interested in. I've got a brochure ..." He wanders back to his office behind the glass partition and roots around in his desk. "Here it is, Alberta College of Art, youth classes. There's a painting class on Saturdays you might want to check out. You could take the bus easily enough."

"Oh. What bus would I take?"

"Just the number one and then transfer. Let me see I have a bus schedule here." He pulls his wallet out and finds a folded paper. "You'd transfer to the number 40 at Fourteenth Street." As he closes his wallet, I see a photo of a beautiful woman, hair in a 1950s bob, creamy skin and dark eyes. He stares at it for a moment and shakes his head, then thrusts the wallet into his back pocket again.

"You know when I came home from the war, the first time I saw her on Main Street in Didsbury, there was this voice in my head that spoke as plain as day." He shakes his head again. "I didn't listen." He stares off into space and I know I shouldn't ask but I do anyway.

"What did it say?"

"What did what say?"

"The voice in your head."

"Oh. It said, 'Walk away, Bob. Just walk away.' I had just come home; the war was over, and the prairie light was so brilliant after the gloom in Holland. I was in the Second Infantry Division, and we were trying to take back the north bank of the River Scheldt ...'" He was off. I settled into washing the brushes and listened.

Margaret tests the curling iron. She licks her finger then touches the iron with a sizzle.

"You can either blow dry the wings out and then use a little hair spray, but if you don't have time to wash your hair you can use a curling iron, like this. Three curls look nice, I think." She wraps a third of my new long bangs around the iron. She waits a minute as steam rises up with the smell of cauterizing protein, and then slowly pulls it down and back. A perfect vertical wave falls softly behind my ear. "Now two more." And she does another one on my temple and another over my ear.

"That looks really good. Your wings look better than Marcie Phelps'," Lindsay says.

"Go get that bag of your clothes from last year, Kelly. It's in the basement on the shelf by the washing machine."

"Oh yeah, I think they would fit Zoe now. Actually, is my jean jacket from last year in there too?"

"I think so. Go see."

I take the bag to the bathroom. I can barely do up Kelly's old 501 Levi's, but they encase my hips and ass in a way completely new to me. The hem covers my sneakers, making my legs look really long. No one would know they were three inches too short. I pull a small pink V-neck t-shirt out of the bag and put it on. In the mirror I suddenly have a figure, breasts and hips and everything. The whole effect would be even better if I stuffed cotton in my bra, and I've been saving a stash from whenever we open a new bottle of vitamins.

Lindsay and I ride home at three because Kelly has to leave for the orthodontist. My old clothes and some more of Kelly's dangle in a shopping bag from the handlebars. The new jeans cut a horizontal wrinkle across the front of my hips when I bend over, but it's totally worth it.

When we get home, cars fill the driveway. My mother arranges a tray of Indian desserts in the kitchen. I sneak a bowl of Gulab jamuns floating in rose water syrup. She looks up and sees me.

"Goodness Zoe, what happened to you? You look so ... uh ... grown up." I guess this doesn't fit with her Hindu ideal of purity or something.

"Kelly's mum did it for *free!* She used to be a hairdresser, you know." A wave of laughter wafts in from the living room where the devotees gather.

"Well, isn't that sweet of her. She is really such a generous soul!" my mother says and picks up the tray and carries it into the living room. I finish my Gulab jamuns and then I peek around the corner. They all stand in a circle starting their "energization exercises." They wear goofy smiles on their faces and drum on their heads with their knuckles. "Awake and ready," they intone. "Awake and ready." As I go upstairs to my room the harmonium begins its organ like droning. The finger cymbals join in, and their voices all rise in a Hindi chant.

Upstairs my father comes out of the bathroom. He's stunk it up again, it always smells like some derivative of coffee when he's done, and he never turns on the fan. He wanders past me and pats me on the head.

"How are you, scoundrel?" he says. I follow him into his study. He walks over to the brick and board bookcase and picks up his industrial sized bottle of Tylenol with codeine. I know that familiar rattle.

"What are you doing, Daddy?"

"Hmmm, what? Oh, I have a headache." He takes two pills and washes them back with a swig of cold coffee. Then he twinkles at me through his heavy black-framed glasses over the brim of the cup.

"'My freedom is a measure of the lengths to which I'll disobey!'"

"Who said that?"

"Hmm, not sure, I think Gandhi or Bob Dylan. Off you go now, honey. I'm going to take a nap."

I close the door and go to my room. My drawing stuff lies on my desk, but I look up to the hoot of the train.

Soon it arrives, barring any view of Josh's house, the sunset light flashing between the speeding cars.

Mr. Bailey tells the class how drawing relates to the different hemispheres of the brain.

"The left brain," he says, "controls verbal reasoning. It thinks in symbols and basically it will just get in the way of your accurately drawing what you see. What you want to do is get into your right hemisphere which only sees *spatial* relationships, but to do that we have to shut the bossy left side up. Today, we're going to give the right hemisphere an advantage by drawing upside down."

"Do you want me stand on my head then, Mr. Bailey?" Josh asks with a big smile, and we all laugh. I try to take Art as an option as often as I can, but this semester Josh registered too. I sit kitty corner from him in the big rectangle of desks that Mr. Bailey arranged and do my best to look cool and calm.

"Yes, Josh. It might be harder for you to talk that way. Everyone else however just needs to rotate this drawing I want you to copy, upside down. Don't turn it right side up until you're finished and then turn it around and see how well you did."

He starts handing around a photocopied line drawing of a man sitting in a chair.

This is the last period of the day. In the morning I got up early and showered and blew dry my hair like Margaret said. She even gave me a bottle of her hairspray to take home, and though I sprayed the mirror the first time by accident, my wings came out perfectly, feathering softly over each temple. I touch them now and the hairspray still holds them, and it's two o'clock. I wear Kelly's jeans and the pink t-shirt. The response has been amazing. Marcie Phelps and Crystal Malloy actually talked to me in the girl's washroom. They asked who had cut my hair and if I had taken a bath in my jeans to get them to fit that well.

I made some joke about taking a bath in my jeans every morning before school and Crystal said: "I didn't know you were so funny. You should come to the party at Daryl Sims's house on Saturday." And I said thanks, but inside I was thinking: "Fuck *you*. You haven't talked to me for the last three years, but today my jeans are tight enough and that makes all the difference?"

I move through the drawing pretty quickly. Mr. Bailey is right; it is easier to see shapes and contours when you copy something upside down. For a while I stay absorbed in my work, but I feel someone watching me. I look up. It's Josh, and it's not his slightly pitying way of registering my existence that I am used to. He tilts his head a bit back and at an angle. When he realizes I've caught him, he looks back down at his work. I do not know what to make of this, so I hand my drawing in to Mr. Bailey. Mr. Bailey says: "You've changed your style, Zoe." And I say: "Well, it's spring, change is in the air." Mr. Bailey laughs and gives me another piece of paper.

"Okay, since some of you finished already, I'm going to explain the next exercise."

I turn around to watch what Mr. Bailey draws on the board, and when he finishes, I turn back, and Josh is looking at me again. This time he gazes right into my eyes. He explores my face like it's some sort of pleasurable leisurely journey, and then gives me this really gentle smile. Everything inside of me goes to goo. Amazingly, I do not blush. I don't think my hands even sweat. I feel strangely removed. Maybe I'm having an out of body experience? I watch myself tilt my chin down and then I look up through my lashes. I bite my lower lip just a bit and run my hand through my wings. My fingers stick in the hairspray but not so anyone would know. Then I go back to drawing, as if Josh Leighton gives me eyeball sex every day of the week.

When the bell rings, everyone gets up and brings their work to Mr. Bailey. Josh stops beside my desk and says something about my drawing being good. And then he says: "Are you walking home right away or are you hanging around? How come I never see you walking back and forth when we both walk the same way to school?"

"I'm walking home," I say.

"I'm walking home too," he says. And then we stand there and smile at each other for a second. I scoop up my binder and am about to head out the door when Mr. Bailey calls me.

"Zoe, why don't you sort through these extra watercolours you've done and take home the ones you'd like to keep." He stands at the table beside his office door. I go over to him, so I don't have to talk too loud.

"Actually, I've got to get going. I'll come in tomorrow during my spare."

Mr. Bailey leans back against the doorframe with his arms folded on his chest. "I'm surprised," he says.

"By what?"

He's saying something, but I don't hear, I'm so focused on Josh leaving the art room.

"I'll see you tomorrow, Mr. Bailey. Have a good night."

I walk down the main hall beside Josh Leighton, not too close but we walk stride for stride with our backpacks on and I know everyone's looking. We leave a ripple of curiosity behind us. I still hover somewhere above myself watching, and I have to say I'm impressed. How, for instance, do I suddenly know enough about basketball to make intelligent conversation?

"In our last game against Churchill it was just way to close," Josh says. "We couldn't afford to be making so many weak passes. We lost our edge. I was getting pretty scared for a while."

"But you pulled it back at the end," I say. "After half time you guys went into the full court press. No one let the pressure off for the rest of the game. It was amazing!"

"Yeah, we did manage to get it back. Hey, I didn't know you knew so much about basketball."

We step outdoors into the late afternoon sun. "Oh, my dad used to take me to games at the university. He played guard in high school."

"Really? Your dad doesn't look all that athletic."

"How do you know what my dad looks like?"

"Oh, I saw you and your parents at last year's awards night." Josh was watching me and my parents?

"You're prettier than you think," he says. At this revelation I feel quite dizzy, and the sidewalk passing beneath my feet does a little sideways shimmy. "Did your dad play university ball?"

"No, I guess he was too short."

"So that's where you get it from."

"What from?"

"The height differential!" He gives my shoulder a gentle shove.

"Hey, that's a low blow." I go to shove him back, but he takes off running. I oblige and chase him.

When we get to the fence, I think maybe he'll say good bye, but instead he vaults over it. Then I watch myself do probably the best chain link fence jump of my life. I get my first foot up really high in the links, my hand on the top rail. I swing up lightly and leap down. We stand there, face to face just two feet apart.

"You're a pretty good fence jumper too."

"Years of practice," I say.

When we get to the train tracks, we rotate and walk towards the trestle. Josh picks up rocks and throws them down the track as we go.

"From the middle, I bet you I could throw a rock right to the other bank. Where the river is narrower, I've thrown a rock clear across."

"Nah," I say, "I don't believe it. You can throw a rock the full length of a train trestle?"

On the trestle now, Josh's legs easily take two ties at a

stride. I try to mince casually and not let the rushing water catch my eyes. When we get to the gravel dyke, he reaches down and takes a handful of rocks from the track. He throws one and it hits the water a metre from the bank.

"Hah!" I say. Josh turns red and throws a bunch of rocks in quick succession. By the end they're all crashing through the dead grass and bushes.

"Let's see you do that."

"I kind of throw like a girl."

"Well, come on, show me."

"No really, I'd rather not."

"Come on."

So, I reach down and pick up a few rocks and throw the first one as hard as I can. I feel a tearing sensation in my shoulder and the rock lands three metres in front of me.

"The mechanics are just off," he says. "Try again and I'll see if I can help you." He cosies up behind me. With his hands he angles my hips correctly. One hand goes up to cup the hand holding the rock, and the other one rests on my shoulder. I feel a slick of electricity wherever we touch. I still can't believe I'm doing this. It's hard to concentrate on the mechanics lesson and evidently Josh thinks so too because after a few rocks we just stand there. I think he's smelling my hair.

Three quick detonations of a train whistle and we both leap in the air. I lurch back and catch my foot on the rail and stumble. The train clears the corner and snakes towards us into view.

"I didn't even feel it coming!" I say. Josh's blue eyes are wide, and his face goes greenish. He turns and takes off, his black hair flashing, heading east towards home as fast as he can. He thinks he can outrun a train like he can throw a rock across the river. I try to keep up to his two ties to my one. But looking back at the train I know we won't make it. Josh keeps running. I put on all the steam I can, don't trip, don't trip, and I somehow manage to grab him by the arm and turn him.

"We won't make it," I yell. "We have to jump!" And I point to the lower beam on the outside of the tracks. Three feet of air stretch between the track and that beam and it's lower than us too. We just have to fix our eyes on it and go, but Josh stares at the train, his face frozen.

"We have to jump!" I yell again, and I turn to the beam, but Josh doesn't move, and I know he can't do it. Beside me stands one of the diagonal braces with its metal latticework. It sure looks like a ladder to me. *If you're not going to jump, you fucking well better climb*, I think. And I grab his hand and pull him behind me.

"Climb!" I shout over my shoulder. I reach my foot over the two feet of air and get it onto the crosspiece and then I'm hand over hand. I never climbed anything so fast in my life. I look down and he follows me up, the train reaches us, a roaring shock wave of sound and vibration. I wrap my arms around the brace and press my cheek hard into the rusted metal. After a while I open my eyes and watch Josh's silky hair below my feet, whipping in the draft coming off the train. It seems to take forever, hours of holding on but it's probably just ten minutes, and then finally I'm watching the tail end of the engine steaming east. It grows smaller and smaller in the distance. The trestle slowly stops vibrating. The tracks give off an occasional electric pinging sound, recovering from the shock of it all.

We climb down, and I start laughing.

"Holy shit!" I say. "I don't think I've ever been so scared!"

But Josh doesn't say anything. His face is petulant, and he won't look at me. He just stares down the river.

"That was a close one," I say again. "I've got to tell my sister. I don't know anyone else who's been on the trestle when a train came except Russell Dobson!"

Finally, Josh turns to me, and he smiles just the way I saw him smile at Marcie Phelps the other day at her locker. He leans in, but I'm thinking: *I saved your ass, aren't you even going to thank me?* His hand brushes the hair off my cheek and then he raises his right eyebrow in this super cool way he has that always makes my knees go weak. And all of a sudden, I know why it looks so familiar. He's borrowed the expression from Captain James T. Kirk. He's channelling fucking William Shatner! The closer he moves the further my skin pulls away. I take a step back.

"Uh, I'm sorry," I say. "I'd better get going. I mean, I'd better get home." I turn, and I run. I clear two ties at a stride, and my heel hits each time with the certainty of a rock splitting the river. I don't stop till I've come to the place where I jump the fence. I look back at him, half his size now standing in the middle of the trestle, his arms hanging by his sides. I raise my hand and wave. There is a moment and then he lifts his hand sort of half way up and waves back.

I get over the fence and it's definitely clumsier than the jump I did half an hour ago. Only when I reach the house do I realize I left my backpack on the dyke between the trestles.

The sun shines with a new heat when I walk up the Crescent. The brown casings of the poplar buds crunch beneath my feet and stick to the bottom of my shoes. Now and then I have to stop and scrape the sticky collection off against the asphalt. Above me the yellow green flames of the new leaves sing and vibrate against the cerulean sky. Cerulean is my favourite blue. I think about a painting that Mr. Bailey showed me by one of the Group of Seven, leaves outlined in red against the light, and now I understand why.

Against my back I feel the weight of the lunch I packed, a cheese sandwich and an orange, and some of my mother's peanut butter sesame energy balls. My drawing pad lies against my shoulder blades like a board, and my pencils from H to B4, rattle quietly in their cedar cigar box with every step.

When I get to Bowness Road, I leave the quiet of the Crescent behind. I wait for a gap in the traffic, and then dash across the street to the bus stop. In a few minutes the Number One pulls up. There is a grinding of gravel and the hissing of air brakes. I climb the stairs and put two quarters in the slot.

"Transfer, please," I say.

Bobcat

The carrot tower lists dangerously aisle wards, as Lucy reaches the twenty-carrot height. She should have stepped it back more as she stacked them up, but the depth of the shelf doesn't allow for the height of her ambition.

"Hey! Look at the hoser killing the pig!" Gabe says.

She turns to the meat department and sees Hank's red face just above the glass case, embroiled in some difficulty with cleaver and bone.

"Shit!" Hank explodes, hopping from foot to foot. He dashes to the sink.

"You ok, Hank?" she calls, but he doesn't hear her over the water. The immense back slackens however, so she figures it's not too bad. Lucy rotates back to her tower. Gabe stands there, greatly tattooed, gap toothed, silver rings overlapping each other like fish scales around the curve of his leathery ear. He smiles, the tower demolished, and all the carrots back in the green plastic crate.

"Hey!"

"Wasn't gonna hold together. Start with a row of butt ends out. Next row, nose end out. Next row, ass end again, see? When you're done, cull the loose onions." An imperceptible wink and he's moved on to tomatoes.

Lucy starts laying the carrots shoulder to shoulder, pulling off stray tops as she goes. Nancy must have come in the office door, because "Little Drummer Boy" starts up on the PA system. Nora's outside rolling up the shutters with the crank. So, another day, a Thursday four days before Christmas, begins at the Bownesian Grocer. Lucy tosses a deformed carrot and revisits her idea of a Seconds and Day-Old shelf. She thinks Gabe might go for it. It's an old idea that's making a comeback in enviro-conscious groceries. She can't believe how much they compost, perfectly good food, and plenty of Bownesians who'd buy a deviant carrot or a bruised tomato at half price. Then, along the same lines but even better, an idea lands in her mind right out of the blue. What about this? What about a kind of freestanding cupboard outside the entrance to the store? She can picture it, on cute long wooden legs, and painted on the cupboard door the motto "Little Free Cupboard." Seconds could be put out for the taking, stuff from the deli that hadn't sold, damaged boxes of this and that. And maybe customers would donate groceries too, like the food bank but tiny. She can picture the curving folksy font: "Little Free Cupboard ... Take what you need, leave what you can." That's amazing! She's so excited she gyrates a little from foot to foot, and hums along with "Little Drummer Boy": *I have no gift to bring ta rump a pum pum, I'll play my drum for you ta rumpa pumpum* ... She'll bring it up with Gabe, maybe when they're packaging the fruit salads in the back bay. It will be more open than closed due to deliveries today, and its minus twenty, snappy and crystalline. On days like today Lucy doesn't take off her toque and wears her down vest under the produce apron. The vest was an amazing score at the Women in Need. Thrifting, as their sign says, is cool. Also, it beats hypothermia.

The misting system goes through its grumbling thunder soundtrack, and Lucy steps back while the jets spray rain over the celery, beets, peppers, and the cauliflower in three-colour varieties including purple and "cheddar." It's been a month since she moved from checkout to produce, a promotion as Gabe's assistant, and she still gets a kick of satisfaction with each tiny storm.

The first customer shows up, the lady who always stops by after the gym, still in her exercise gear. Lucy tries to imagine a life like that. "Working out" each morning, then shopping for organic produce to turn into healthy ethnic fair for your rich husband and adorable children. Last week Lucy and the woman discussed the ripeness of avocadoes to make brown rice sushi, California rolls. While Lucy layers up row number six, a nose out row, the woman picks out the fattest bunch of kale and some green onions. Lucy eyes the leather driving gloves in her shopping basket, periwinkle blue, and compares them to her own fingerless wool gloves. She'd bought them two sizes too big at the Women in Need, then boiled them so the fibres locked together. 'Felting,' it was called. Then she cut off the fingers above the second knuckle and finished each raw edge with a different color of yarn. Burnt orange, mossy green, a surprising hit of pale pink. Lucy just got a book about felting from the Bowness Library and she's full of ideas for repurposing old sweaters. She and the woman smile at each other, worlds apart, but also not.

"How's your day so far?" Gym Lady asks.

"Good. Can't complain. How about you?"

"Well, you won't believe what I almost ran into in the driveway this morning!"

"What?"

"The Bowness bobcat! It's so cocky! It didn't even hurry, just kept strolling down the sidewalk heading east."

"I was watching about that on the news," Lucy says. "They got a film of it sitting on top of Ray Nielson's pigeon coop. Ray wasn't so happy!"

Gabe, piling tomato boxes onto the produce trolley, looks over.

"Well, he should worry about his birds. Once a bobcat makes up its mind it don't give up. Specially a female."

"My cat's been locked up for a week, but that's all you can do, I guess. I'm too scared to let her out." Lucy finishes up the final row.

"I know. I'm watching out for my dachshund! He'd be a sausage snack for a bobcat. I phoned Animal Control, but they said they won't trap it. I guess a new one would move in as soon as the old one leaves. They told me to spray it with a hose. Like that's much use in December. Or make a lot of noise to chase it off. Mind you, it's so beautiful. And isn't it amazing that wildlife just roams around Bowness? It reminds me of growing up in the Kootenays, with bears and bobcats all over the place. How do you know it's a female?" Gym Lady turns to Gabe.

"A friend of mine spotted its den, up behind Bowness Park in the Douglas Fir. She had three kits this spring. She's probably still taking them food."

Lucy's phone pings in her back pocket and she pulls it out to check the text.

Guess what? Me and the kid are coming to Cowtown for Christmas!

Oh shit. Lucy rams it back into her pocket. Gym Lady's saying something about probable bobcat hunting ranges, but she can't focus. The carrots are done. What was next? Oh right, onions.

At ten fifteen Lucy, Nora, Hank, and Nancy huddle on the bench on the east façade of the Bownesian Grocer. They produce a cumulous cloud of smoke in the morning sun and warm their hands around cardboard cups of coffee from the Shop and Go. Lucy is a beginner 'cloud chaser,' and she's still not sure if her vaping journey, as the guy at the One Stop Vape Shop says, is working out or not. Nancy's convinced most of the staff to switch to vaping for safety reasons. Lucy practices her slow inhale to the back of the mouth, then the deeper pull to the lungs. It's a longer rhythm than the quick sucking inhale with a cigarette. She's an MTL, mouth-to-lung vaper, unlike Hank who's a DL, direct lung guy. The hit of nicotine is more instant with DL, but Lucy tells Hank he's missing out on the mouth feel, the density and flavour aspects. Oh well, some people are only about the destination, not the journey. Today she's trying cinnamon flavour, and it feels good, not sucking in all that toxic tar anymore.

"I think I'll start building my own coils," Hank says.

"It's cheaper. When are you getting a dripper, Lucy? You need something with variable wattage, so you can really fine tune it. You know, find your sweet spot." Lucy eyes her vape pen. It cost her sixty bucks and she's happy with the small size for her purse. She turns to Nancy, her manager.

"When do you think its ok to end an old friendship, Nancy? Did you ever have to do that?"

Nancy leans back and takes a long pull on her dripper. She always looks so put together. Lucy admires her backcombed ponytail and cat's eye liner. It's so cold working in the loading dock, that Lucy has given up on hair and sticks to a floppy toque. Not that she's abandoned makeup mind you. Her eyes are big and brown, and she accentuates them with dusky shadow and a little mascara.

"How old a friendship are you talking? Like from high school? Junior high?"

"No, elementary. Grade three! We've been friends so long it's almost like we're related."

"Old friends are the best friends," Nora says, taking the cigarette from her mouth and blowing sideways over her shoulder. "You'll never get that history back. I know. I fell out with my best friend. Actually, she's my cousin. I don't know how to fix it now. Still regret it, 'specially round Christmas."

"What if your friend really messed up though?"

"Well, was she drinking? My cousin and I were pissed. All sorts of stupid shit happens when you're pissed. It's better to just forget about that stuff, that's what I say."

Well, that's true, Lucy thinks, *they'd had some beers.* Cherise was going through a bad time since she'd ended it with Chase's dad. And what an asshole he'd been, thrown her against the fridge that time. And he'd nearly killed their husky, hanging him up by the choke collar. Thank God, she'd managed to get away before he did worse.

"Jesus was all about forgiveness, about turning the other cheek," Nancy, who's recently gone Baptist, says. She sinks deeper into the fluffy scarf swathing her neck and blows peppermint steam into the sideways blinding winter sun. "And Nora's right about Christmas."

Ping

What exactly is your address? What's the name of the community? Brentwood?

Having stuffed her fingerless gloves in the produce apron pocket, Lucy picks up a kiwi. She makes a nick with her paring knife, and catching the furry skin between blade and thumb, convinces it to part with the green translucent flesh underneath. This is the third text in an hour and she's pretending she's busy. What would Cherise know anyhow? She can tell her that staff aren't allowed to check their phones at work.

"Gabe?"

"Yeah?"

"How do you know if someone's flirting with you, or if they're just having fun? I mean, as a guy, how do you know when a woman's hitting on you in a serious way?"

"You're asking me?"

"Sure, you're a dude with experience."

"*Old*, you mean."

"Well, you're pretty fit. I bet you've had lots of, uh, opportunities ..."

Gabe smiles with all the spaces between his teeth and flexes his muscle. The sailing ship beneath the tattered V-neck, rocks on the waves of his upper pec. He plunges his knife into a honeydew, cracks it open and scrapes the seeds into the compost bucket with a plastic paddle.

"When it's fun, and when it's serious? Well, that's an intuitive thing, right? It moves from out *here*." He flutters the sticky paddle around his perimeter. "Just a playful electricity, you know. But when it's serious it moves to *here*." He grabs his apron at his lower belly in two fists, thrusts down. "Everything else cuts out. I'm trying to remember my wilder days. It's adrenalin and total focus, and you can only see *her*." Lucy drops the slippery peeled kiwi into the stainless-steel bowl, and reaches staring, for another one.

"Wow! Okay then!"

"I was a bit of a slayer in my day, till Jennie showed up."

"But that's not what I mean, Gabe. What does the *woman* do to show, you know, to show that she's into him?"

"Why do you ask? You're a girl, why ask me?" He cuts the halves into quarters, pares off the rind in two strokes and dices each section.

"How many kiwis should I do?"

"Two bags, and then whatever's getting too ripe. What needs using up?"

"Pears, I guess."

"So, what's up?"

"Oh, this friend of mine. I'd swear she's ... but maybe it's just harmless fun, right? I don't want to get all jelli or anything. But Derek's *so* clueless."

"Derek's a good guy and smart, don't get me wrong. Not everyone makes it as a journeyman plumber. But there's some Fred Flintstone, hey?"

Lucy snorts as she laughs and hooks another bag of kiwi fruit open with her paring knife.

"It's true! He's so smart, and then he's so dumb!"

"So, who's hitting on Derek?"

Lucy grits her teeth and keeps working on the tricky fuzzy-skinned fruit.

"I don't even want to talk about it. It makes me feel sick. Just tell me if I'm nuts. Last time we got together with her and her little boy Chase. Her name's Cherise. She just, I don't know, *laughed* too much. I mean, his jokes aren't actually that funny. And she stood, she just stood *too close*."

"How close is too close?"

Lucy holds her hands apart by three feet, brings them slowly together. Gabe cocks a noncommittal eyebrow at two feet.

"No," Lucy says. "It was closer than that. It was like one foot, and she was staring up at him all doe eyed like Bambi. I saw her when she was supposed to be bringing in the salad. She kept asking him to help her in the kitchen. Derek, like you say, didn't seem to catch on. And she wanted him to tell her all about *plumbing*, give me a break. And when he showed her this section of pipe that he'd soldered as a demo, she kept *stroking* it and saying what great work he did. It made me want to hurl."

"Ahha! Stroking his pipe ... *Stroking's* a big one. When a girl wants to uh, you know, she starts stroking shit, yeah. And tells you you're such a dude. I remember. And they play with their hair a lot. Did she play with her hair?"

"Well yes, she did! She kept running her hands through her hair!" Lucy's freezing. She takes a deep breath and fishes the last kiwi out of the bag. "She's my best friend, since we were nine. We went to the same elementary in Red Deer."

Gabe wipes his hands on his apron and pulls a box of mandarin oranges closer. "Does she have a boyfriend?"

"No, she dumped him. He was an asshole."

"And a kid?"

"Yeah, a little boy, four years old."

"Ah. Well there you go."

"But she's my best friend!"

"All's fair in love and war, right? Isn't that what they say?"

"The bobcat walked past my fence last night," Rob, with his weathered face, says. His long hair reaches to his hips now.

"Not framing today?' Gabe takes in the tattered black sweats, a change from his friend's usual canvas work pants.

"I've got a few days between houses in Aspen Meadows, and I can't say I mind. The thermometer's been stuck at minus nineteen and doesn't want to budge."

"They can't make you work after minus twenty,

right?" Lucy lays out the plastic containers of fruit salad in the deli cooler. "It's not so bad for Derek, at least he's working in a roughed in building with a heater."

"What's he do again?"

"Journeyman plumber!"

"Well that's a good choice," Rob says. "I wasn't thinking when I picked framing. It's a young man's job and I'm getting too old."

"Another lady saw the bobcat this morning, hey Lucy? Walking right down Thirty-third Street. She said she was heading east on the sidewalk, just like she owned it."

Rob searches through the packaged meals put together by the Bownesian's own chef, Terrry. It's a toss-up between the large breakfast, or brisket, mashed potatoes, and broccoli. He decides to take one of each. Talking about the cold just makes him hungrier.

"Well she does own it! What would *you* do if you bumped noses with her on the sidewalk? Guess I'd just step aside and say, 'good morning'! She doesn't have a regular route like the coyotes though. They stick to their old paths. But a bobcat's more spontaneous. Her prey must be getting scarce, so she's hunting in town."

Lucy goes home for a late lunch at two. Their rented duplex on 32nd Avenue is only a five-minute walk, and she likes the quiet. She sits cross legged in the sun in front of the sliding glass doors. Her grey tabby Ziggy claws up the back of the sofa with her tail puffed up and all toes splayed, cat bell tinkling. At the top she crouches with one of those psychotic cat looks, her butt in the air, dekes left, dekes right, and leaps to the floor. She's got serious cabin fever. Lucy considers the tiny stucco bungalow with its crabapple tree across the street. In a few years, if they're careful, they can put a deposit down and buy something of their own. Something like that. Small, but with a garden. Even better if it had a basement suite to help with the mortgage. *You're so lucky. Chase and I won't ever get out of this basement shit hole.* She was lucky. She was lucky to even be renting this south facing above grade apartment. The microwave beeps and she stands up to retrieve her defrosted bean burrito. Ziggy ricochets around the living room, going so fast she barely makes the corner as she slides across the linoleum and tears down the hall.

Lucy takes Derek's spin rod from the corner and sits back down. The sun catches in the greenery of the little fir they bought last night at the Scout Hall. For a twelve-dollar tree it was pretty bushy. It rests in a bucket of water and smells so fresh and Christmassy. She'll put it in the stand tonight. The cat races back into the living room. Lucy casts the fishing rod and then takes a bite of burrito. She's trying to wear Ziggy out, by getting her to chase a feather she's tied with a split shot to the end of the line. She casts the feather right across the room and slowly reels in the cat, pouncing all the way. To be honest, the dinner with Cherise and Chase in the fall was the third time. The fishing trip in July was the second. With the bikini. And so what, right? It had been a hot day, but still, maybe some cut offs and a t-shirt once they'd finished with swimming?

Because her tits really were mind blowing, stretched out in the raft all afternoon, with her best friend and her friend's boyfriend teaching her little guy to fish. And now it was this ongoing thing, how Chase had never had a better time than that weekend rafting and fishing with Derek. How Derek better not break the little guy's heart, because all Chase talks about now was going fishing with him again in the spring. *Yeah*, Lucy said. *Kids always love Derek. He can't help himself. He goes all out if there's a kid around.* Since the dinner at Cherise's place in Red Deer, Lucy's been doing her best to distance, to make excuses, to be unavailable.

Ping

Lucy turns it over and looks. Cherise is digging deep now and pulling out old photos. There they are in grade eight, Lucy's toothy grin and big dark eyes, Cherise arching her neck, aping a pout. Both of them wear the requisite thick black eyeliner, and those plastic headbands that dug into your scalp. Doing their best, with their skinny straight hipped bodies to "walk it out." Lucy remembers a Saturday bingeing on Unk's rapper tune, and how sore her abs were for a week from the hip flailing dance move, kind of like doing the twist but deeper and looser.

Ping

A photo of them cheek to cheek, wet hair, the eyeliner, sunburnt noses and cheekbones. Lucy casts the weighted feather again for Ziggy. The nostalgic scent of creosote wafts from the tarry train track ties in the August sun, the same sun that bakes her halter topped back. Lucy screwed up the courage to jump shrieking from the bottom deck of the trestle, the cold green closing over her head. The halter top washing up to her armpits. She'd pulled it back into place while trying not to drown. Lying panting on the hot river rocks to warm up, she watched the kids in silhouette on the trestle, and they all stared at one person: Cherise, on the very top beam. Arms raised against the blue, blue sky, she turned right and left. Watch me! And then the amazing silent swooping swan dive, and how they'd all shouted when she'd cut into the water, pretty much like a knife. Cherise drove eighty to Lucy's sixty on country range roads. It's fun, she'd said, like swimming around in the gravel. Lucy Winton, Cherise McCaig's best friend. She eats the last bite of bean burrito and sucks the taco sauce off her thumb before standing up.

"Kitty, kitty, kitty ..." The grey tabby follows her to the bedroom, pouncing on her socks with each step, the cat bell on her collar jingling. Crazy cat needed a good night of mouse-ing to empty her batteries. Lucy takes a handful of kibble from the quart jar on top of the dresser, and drops it with the familiar musical plash into Ziggy's bowl. As soon as the cat's leapt to the top of the dresser Lucy scoots out of the bedroom, shutting the door behind her. In the kitchen she shrugs into her parka and pulls on her battered ankle boots. She takes a look around the sunny spare room. Hopefully she can decorate the tree tonight. There were tinsel stars at the dollar store, and she could cut paper snowflakes, and maybe string popcorn? Maybe she should make pompom balls with her scraps of yarn? She could string them together into a long bunting, or maybe just hang them individually. In the freezer waits the stuffed turkey breast and the bag of cranberries. It's a toss-up between salad or Brussels sprouts, and you can make good gravy with a bouillon cube, seeing how you don't get much in the way of drippings off a turkey breast. *I can always say I lost my phone*, Lucy thinks, squinting into the westering sun on her walk back to the Bownesian, a cloud of cinnamon steam trailing behind her.

Brightly shone the moon that night, though the frost was cruel ... She pushes the produce trolley through the swinging doors and passes by ice cream and frozen fruit. The first time, did that even count? Cherise was such a live wire. Maybe she was like that with everyone? Lucy turns left after the coffee grinding machine and runs her eyes over the array of produce. It's pretty picked over, but they've got a huge shipment to unpack for this pre-Christmas weekend. She pulls out the first box and tips the Cremini mushrooms, balancing the lip on the side of the produce shelf, and scoops them out with her hand. You have to go slow, so the rubbery fungi don't bounce all over the place. Did any of it actually count? It wasn't like Cherise had *propositioned* Derek or anything. They had been drinking that night, the second time, and it was just a month after Cherise's break up from dick head. Maybe she'd taken the hint, registered Lucy's cold shoulder, and now the photos of the two of them was a message, Lucy and Cherise, best friends since grade three. Hopefully at Christmas people think deeper about things, about the sanctity of stuff like friendship. *Bring me flesh and bring me wine, bring me pine logs hither.* Lucy loves this carol and starts to sing under her breath. *Page and monarch, forth they went, forth they went together* ... Christmas joy floods her. She'll call Cherise tonight, and explain that her phone needed a new battery or something. She starts unpacking a box of butter lettuce. And she can't forget to talk to Gabe about her idea for the Little Free Cupboard. How incredible if they could get that up before Christmas?

Ping

It's Derek!

Want to meet me and Jay at The Place for pizza?

"I think it's your friend," Derek says. "How'd she get my number?" He pushes his phone across the table towards her and takes another slice of pizza. Lucy turns the phone over. A photo of little Chase, grinning in a goofy elf hat. *Hey! Lucy says we're crashing your place for Christmas! But she's not answering her phone, maybe she lost it? Just let me know your address. It's crazy, but I've never seen your new place!*

"Oh ho! *Rafting* Cherise?" Jay says. "If her little guy's gonna wear an elf suit, I wonder what *she'll* be wearing?" He and Derek snort into their beer mugs.

By the time they get home after shooting some pool at Hexter's, it's nine o'clock. Derek dumps all his work gear inside the door: his decal covered hard hat, steel toed boots, tattered ski gloves, the safety vest with dayglo reflective strips.

"I gotta hit the hay, babe," Derek says yawning. He's been up since five, double checking rough ins for an early morning pour. He sheds clothes in a trail to the bedroom, the mustard canvas work pants, long john's, wool socks.

"I'll come in a bit, I need to tire out Ziggy or she'll attack us all night."

"Ziggy? I think she went out when I brought the stuff in from the truck."

"What do you mean, she *went out*? She's not *allowed* out, right? Remember the bobcat? Why do you think she's acting so wrangy? I've been keeping her in all week because they're spotting that bobcat all over Bowness!"

"Oh babe, I'm so tired. I can't think about this. I've got to go to bed!" He walks into the bedroom and shuts the door behind him.

"Fuck *me*." Lucy grips her head and pulls off her floppy toque. God, she's tired of wearing a hat all the time. She wants to take a hot bath, but she'd better keep checking the door for the cat. It's really cold, minus twenty at least. In a few minutes Ziggy will be there crouched on the mat wanting to come in.

Turning, she walks through the kitchen, down the four steps to the landing and opens the door to the frosty night. There's a halo around the moon. Doesn't that mean snow? "Kitty, kitty, kitty! Here kitty, kitty, kitty!" She listens for the tinkle of Ziggy's cat bell, looks left to the street and right to the back yard along the narrow walkway beside the neighbour's fence. Silence, no tinkle, no answering 'mrow?' "Kitty, kitty, kitty?" Nothing. Lucy shuts the door and walks back upstairs. She can hear Derek already snoring from the bedroom. He always snores after a few beers.

In the kitchen she fills the kettle and picking up Derek's phone from the counter, studies the photo of Chase in the elf hat. The little boy has Cherise's long hazel eyes, but blond hair like his father, dick head. She drops a Sleepy Time teabag into a cup and adds a squirt of honey from the honey bear. From her memory come the strains of "Good King Wenceslas," but thinner now, and from a distance. *Sire, the night is darker now, and the wind blows stronger. Fails my heart, I know not how, I can go no longer.* She retrieves milk from the fridge, pours some into her tea and walks to the couch. Lucy curls in the corner and pulls the fleece throw around her. She drinks her tea and burrows down, listening with one ear for that faint but insistent meow. *Mark my footsteps, my good page ...* This was Lucy's favourite part, the green footsteps melted in the snow. She tries to remember the exact words that she's heard over and over this month on the sound system. The furnace rumbles and kicks in. She's warm now from the tea and the blanket, *heat was in the very sod which the saint had printed.*

Lucy wakes with a jerk and sits bolt upright. Ziggy screams. The yowling, wailing, hissing shriek of a cat in battle.

She struggles out of the blanket and knocks over her cup. "Ziggy!" In a minute she's down the stairs, unlocking and pulling open the door. "Ziggy!" she looks right and left but can't see her, and Ziggy screams again, and screams like she really, really means it. Lucy leans down and grabs Derek's hard hat in one hand, a steel toed boot in the other and runs sock footed over the crusted snow. One more warbling shriek and Lucy spots them in the moonlight; the bobcat hunkers on top of the neighbour's fence, and Ziggy stares up, crouched on the ground below her. They are suspended in eye to eye combat, and the tabby fights for her life with nothing but that yowl and her refusal to blink. The bobcat's upper lip twitches revealing a momentary canine, and she gives off a little hiss.

"Oh Jesus ..." Lucy says. *Spray it with water, make a lot of noise.* For a moment she's as frozen as the soles of her feet melting into the snow, but then she starts screaming. "*Get out! Get out! Get the fuck out of my yard!*" And she hurls Derek's heavy boot and then the hardhat for good measure. With the first shout the bobcat somehow swivels inside her fur, turns her face away, and then, just vanishes. The boot sails impotently after her, disappearing on the other side of the fence. The hard hat bounces on the snow.

"*Oh Ziggy! Oh kitty!*" The cat, puffed to three times her normal volume, rises to her paws and on stiff legs, stalks slowly back to her owner. Once scooped up, Ziggy buries her head against Lucy's neck and purrs and purrs. Lucy finally registers the pain in her feet, and holding the cat tight, runs for the door. Inside she locks the deadbolt. Nothing's changed. Derek's snores can be heard steady and faint from the bedroom. Jesus Christ, Ziggy could have been eaten and he'd have slept right through it! She stands there on the landing and just holds onto her fiercely vibrating cat.

Ping

It's Derek's phone in the kitchen. Lucy goes upstairs and sits down at the table, settling the cat on her lap.

It's starting to look a lot like Christmas ... And another photo of Chase in the elf hat, this time grinning in a tub of bubbles. Ziggy wriggles and she puts her down on the floor, then drops her head into her hands and closes her eyes. She looks up, heart pounding, and with the tip of one finger she types.

Very cute. She adds several Santa Claus emojis. *But if Chase is just wearing an elf hat, I'm wondering what you'll be wearing for Christmas ...?* She feels sick to her stomach but adds the winking smiley face emoji. *Come on, come on, show me what you're made of.* Nothing happens for five minutes. Then the little grey thought bubble pops up with the three dots that blink in succession. Over in Red Deer, Cherise types:

Ping

Ho, ho, ho ...!

Ping

And it's a photo of Cherise in the elf hat, and not much else but what appears to be a wife beater, her tits lolling to either side, nipples telegraphing through the almost transparent knit. Fuck, and she's winking back.

Ping

How do you like my rack of lamb??? Lucy contemplates her best friend's breasts. What on Earth to say? Finally, she types:

Actually, this is Lucy. You're right about the Ho. And you need to make different plans for Christmas.

Her heart's stops pounding and now she's only numb.

With Derek's phone she Googles 'how to block a caller on an iPhone,' and systematically blocks Cherise's contact on Derek's phone, and then on hers. Next, she does her Instagram and Facebook, and both of their emails. Luckily, they don't have a landline.

When it's all done, Lucy stands up in her wet socks. She goes back to the door, pulls on boots this time, steps out into the minus twenty crackling night, and closes the door behind her. She walks through the back yard to the alley, opens the neighbour's gate as quietly as possible, and retrieves Derek's boot from their bed of raspberry canes up against the fence. Back in the postage stamp yard behind the duplex, Lucy leans down and picks up Derek's hard hat and plops it on her head. My *yard*, she thinks, looking around her as her hand sticks momentarily to the freezing door knob. Next summer she'll have pots of tomato plants and herbs. On the landing she hangs the hard hat on the coat rack, then picks up all his other gear and hangs it up too: the safety vest, his thick work coat. She lines the steel-toed boots up neatly beside her own ankle boots, and their two pairs of runners, and tucks his decrepit ski gloves into his coat pocket with satisfaction. Her gift to him this Christmas waits in a bag under the bed: *proper* waterproof, breathable winter work gloves. They'd cost her the moon at Mark's Work Wearhouse.

Upstairs she scoops up the canvas pants, long johns, the wool socks, flicking off light switches as she goes. My *upstairs sunny apartment*, she thinks. My *Charlie Brown Christmas tree, waiting in a bucket of water.* She throws all his clothes into the hamper in the bathroom, strips off hers as well, and finally the clammy socks. Ziggy appears around the door and watches as she brushes her teeth. She looks at herself naked in the mirror, her small but lovely breasts. My *really quite nice tits*. Entering the bedroom of snores, Lucy feeds the cat her last handful of kibble for the day, and then crawls between the covers. Derek rolls from his back to his side and pulls her into the warmth. "Lou," he mutters into her hair. My *beery but really very decent boyfriend*. Ziggy leaps up onto the bed. She lifts the blanket up forming the customary cave, and the cat curls silky and exhausted against her chest. My *tough enough, incredibly brave kitty*.

Lucy still reverberates with all of it. Lying there, she tries to block out her friend's smiling face behind her shoulder, the touch of Cherise's hands as she French braided Lucy's hair. And the arcing silent swan dive keeps going in replay. In the freezer waits the stuffed turkey breast and the bag of real cranberries. She'll buy mealy brown potatoes and mash them with sour cream and chopped green onions. She'll do a really beautiful salad with a pomegranate and one of those Asian Pears Gabe just brought in. And tomorrow she'll stop at the Women in Need and hopefully find some used merino sweaters, so that on Boxing Day she can start with her felted pillow project for the couch. Blissfully, Derek doesn't snore on his side. Lucy meanders amongst popcorn strings, tinsel Dollar Store stars, pompoms, maybe little gingerbread men to hang on the tree? Sandwiched in warmth between Derek and Ziggy, she stares out the dark window, and snow crystals begin to twinkle and spiral under the streetlight.

Mrs. Mobach

Mrs. Mobach went missing the first week of February. Had it been Monday when Jem got his four-month vaccinations? She couldn't remember anything else to mark the time. Each morning she woke up and tamped down the panic in her stomach. No deadlines, no project of any more importance than the thirty paltry domestic tasks she could do that day. Did it matter if a closet got organized or the laundry folded? Her son lay still sleeping, his black head tucked snuggly under her chin, his spine rounded into the hollow of her breastbone, the reason she could not leave, knew she would not leave even though she talked of daycare and returning to work come September.

Nick had gone in early and left her to sleep, and now silence fills the house. She watches heavy wet flakes of snow falling against the peach stucco of the butcher's house across the street. She would get up and toast a bagel and drink tea. Easing herself away from the tiny satisfying body of her baby, she wedges a pillow against his back to replace her presence and sits and watches him sleep. His eyelids faintly violet, dark lashes lying on his creamy skin like feathers. Little jailor. Inexplicable Buddha.

Mrs. Mobach lived in the corner house two blocks up

the hill from the white bungalow they bought when they found out she was pregnant. The trendy downtown loft would be too small, and the downstairs neighbour had started banging on the ceiling with a broom whenever Rosco barked. They needed a yard and the space to make noise, but on a budget. Montgomery, a blue-collar neighbourhood, was a mix of seniors, working class families, dodgy rentals and student dives. Everyone lived in matchbox-sized bungalows. When they moved in, she painted the rooms bright colours. There was nothing else to do with them. Nothing of architectural interest in an eight-foot square box, and colour at least was free. No more than a white can of paint.

The Mobachs' bungalow was a particularly cute and immaculate box, the siding painted a golden brown, with a piercing green trim. A miniature log cabin bird feeder, painted to match, crowned a post at the front gate. Mr. Mobach, lean and grey in cowboy boots, went for his walk past her living room window every morning precisely at ten. His wife, softly plump, her short curls as white as goose down, could be spotted working at the kitchen window. A sign by the back door, a wooden cutout of a cartoon crow with his wing around a feminine chicken read: "An Old Crow and a Cute Chick Live Here." She imagined Mr. Mobach cut it out himself with his jigsaw in the basement. It kept watch over the back garden and its vast crop of spinning whirligigs. The garden lay in humps of muddy slush and ice now, most of the wind vanes and whirligigs half buried or frozen at the axle. Only the plywood Tweety Bird ran on dauntless, fixed to the top of the laundry pole.

She pulls on jeans and a sweater after her shower and brushes the tangles out of her wet hair. Jem starts mewing and smiles at her when she comes into view over the pillow. *Clever child only smiles for me.* The first time it happened he looked comically embarrassed, his face forming into a crooked grin, cracking her heart in two. Dry diaper, warm socks. The beige pants and red snap-at-the crotch turtleneck? Red might be bad luck today. The fuzzy blue suit with embroidered penguins? *I'm losing my mind*, she thinks.

In the kitchen Jem sucks the milk out of her left breast while she drinks tea and butters her bagel with her right hand. Nick phones sounding tired. He hasn't caught up after the all-nighter for the Carewest proposal, and now they want him to stay late to finish the specs. How's Jem? Has he tried to roll over again? How are you? I'm fine, she lies. His voice is too quiet when he got this tired.

She opens the paper, damp from the snow, and reads the headlines: "Montgomery Senior Still Missing—Search Continues—Day Three." There is a picture of two policemen and a German Shepherd combing through an alley. She knows the spot, behind the Seven Eleven on Beaufort Road, only six blocks from her house. A quote from Mr. Mobach says his wife went to the store, but when he came inside from shovelling the walk, her keys and purse were on the hall table where she always left them.

Everyone in the neighbourhood was looking, had an eye out. It was always on your mind, the mail lady said to her yesterday. Janet Bane next door said she forgot about it when she got to work, but once she got home, she remembered and couldn't stop thinking about it. She switches

Jem to her right breast. Should she and Jem meet her old work friends for lunch? No, what did they have to talk about anymore after all? Nothing really, and her friend's voice grows more patiently strained every time she calls. She'll take Jem to the library, buy some groceries, and walk the dog. She makes a list of the three tasks with a little box beside each to tick it off. It is ten after ten, and Mr. Mobach wouldn't be walking by today.

She starts taking Rosco places she wouldn't normally go, back alleys and isolated stretches of park. It would worry Nick if he knew, so she doesn't tell him. She figures she'd covered the east half of Montgomery pretty thoroughly, every parking lot and alley, and behind the storage warehouse. She even climbed up and looked into dumpsters while Jem slept in the baby carrier on her chest, zipped inside her coat.

The hovering ceiling of cloud hasn't lifted for a week and more wet snow falls now, piling up on the frozen rutted stuff underneath. It is day six and they've called off the search. The thought of the old woman picked up by some psychopath moving through is unbearable. Maybe Mrs. Mobach was senile, she hadn't ever talked to her after all, just seen her working bent over in her garden. Maybe she'd caught a bus and been swallowed up in the labyrinth of city transport. But surely someone would have noticed and talked to her?

Today is the last day she would do this. Today the

final task, to walk the perimeter of the entire community along the riverbank until she comes to the highway bridge, and then down the chain link fence and the strip of city land along Shaganappi Trail. She would keep Rosco on leash. He can't be trusted near river ice or traffic.

So, they walk the bike path along the river till it ends and then she follows a trail through the snow behind the trailer park, empty of campers now. It had been a very cold winter and the river froze all the way across, heaving and piling up on itself, dirty yellow ice. She keeps breaking through the frozen crust of snow, while little Rosco skitters along on top.

She stops to rest. The river ice creaks, a woodpecker hammers insistently. In the distance she can hear the highway, and the wet snow keeps falling softly down. She takes her toque off and shakes away the snow, so it wouldn't fall inside her collar. Coming to the pedestrian walkway under the Hextall Bridge, she leans on the railing, looking at the black water slipping under the ice. This is the only open water along the whole stretch. Leading to that open water, boot prints march steadily to the edge of the ice. The prints scuff and shift at the end as if in momentary hesitation, but there are no boot prints that turn. No prints that walk back to the bank. And then she knows, and there is nothing to do but go home and phone the police.

She turns away from the river and back to the streets of little bungalows and starts to cry, weeping at first, but by the time she reaches Eighteenth Avenue, heaving sobs come from her belly and she can't stop. Snot runs down over her lips. She ducks into an alley and backs behind the corner of someone's garage. Rosco chews an ice ball from between his toes, stopping now and then to give her a worried look, and she's woken Jem now squirming inside her coat. Finally finished and finding a crumpled Kleenex in her pocket, she blows her nose and swabs her eyes with the sleeve of her coat. She decides to cut uphill through the park. It is a steep but quicker route home.

When she gets to the park, she lets Rosco off leash. As she climbs the snowfall finally peters out, and the sun manages to escape and blaze out for a moment under the ceiling of cloud just before it slips below the horizon. In the glare the hill turns blinding white and the poplars flame golden against the slate blue sky. She squints up, and over the crest of the hill sees a funny thing, someone's head and shoulders rising, gradually a whole person, as whoever it is comes down the hill towards her and into view. A tall woman, she sees now, pushing a huge jogging stroller, slaloming down in big turns so it won't get away from her. The woman makes her way down and comes to a stop at the bottom of the hill right beside her.

"Hello!"

"Hi."

"You live around here, don't you?" the woman says. "I've seen you walking. My name is Catherine." She smiles like the newly arrived sun. Three children under the age of five, sardined into the stroller, survey her calmly.

"Uh, my name's Maddie," she says.

"How old is your baby? Isn't he beautifully fat!"

"Just four months."

The woman, Catherine, studies her for a minute and says: "I'm a horribly honest person. Whatever I think just comes right out of my mouth. And I have to say right now you look kind of desperate. I think you need to come to my house pretty soon for tea."

Maddie laughs.

"Yes," she says. "Yes, I think I do."

Maddie phones the police and they match the boot prints to the ones in the Mobachs' yard. But there is no way to find her body till the river breaks up. When they do find her in April, she'd drifted all the way to the Crowchild Trail Bridge. Mr. Mobach moves away, and it makes Maddie ache every time she walks past the log cabin birdfeeder. She and Ann Birch, a woman she'd met on the corner smiling calmly while her toddler sits waist deep in a puddle of snow melt, talk about it. Ann says maybe Mrs. Mobach had been sick, gotten some bad news from her doctor. Maybe she'd been diagnosed with cancer or dementia. You never know what's going on in people's lives.

"Lucky we're only a block away." Ann laughs as the toddler staggers out of the puddle. "How much do you think that diaper weighs now?"

More and more, a funny thing starts to happen with Maddie. She'd be in the house, Jem throwing food around the kitchen from his high chair, the air smelling of some member of the cabbage family she hadn't managed to locate in the back of the fridge, toys and dishes and books in every direction. It leaves Maddie downright suicidal with the mundanity of it all. And then, just occasionally something inside of her would shift.

A shaft of sunlight might slide across the floorboards rendering them to gold for a moment, illuminating the dust bunnies into asteroids for the baby's outstretched pudgy hand. Or the cord of the vacuum cleaner might, suddenly, cease to be a tangle and transform itself instead into a languorous hieroglyphic. A symbol for the freedom she had that day: to grow her little boy, to walk with her friend in the park, to smell the weather, just for a while, like a child.

Archimedes

She stands under the spruce clutching the cardigan tight to keep from freezing. The sun illuminates the Gothic arched interior of the old tree, glittering on airborne ice crystals. Wind whips through and showers her with snow and dead needles. He grins down at her, a good fifteen feet up, an eighty-year-old man in snow pants and a toque refusing to listen. Another coughing fit, and he wraps his arm around the trunk till he's done. It's a miracle he never fell. Her teeth clatter together between her lips. She's been trying to get him down for the last ten minutes. Snow melts inside her slippers.

"For the love of God, Saul, come down now! It's time for breakfast! I'm cold!"

"But there's a bird nest!" He points above him to the messy two-foot wide conglomeration of twigs. "I'm almost there!"

"It's the owl's nest. They'll attack you, I swear, if you get too near. I wouldn't blame them if they did!" Wheedling now. "Come. I made bacon, and if you don't get there quick, I'm eating all of it ..." Mollie covers her head from the shower of needles as he flips onto his belly and starts his descent.

Across the breakfast table she watches his hands, long, square tipped fingers, wasting now, dark with age spots. His spoon vibrates a few inches above the table. Mollie picks up her egg in her own arthritic claw, small and pale but steady enough. She whacks off the top of the egg with a knife, puts it in its eggcup and reaches for the salt. Outside the sun glances off the snow. It streams through the windows into the breakfast nook. The thermometer reads minus 25 Celsius. Today after the doctor's appointment she must get the walk shovelled and finally put away the Christmas decorations. Piles of mail and books, things needing attending to, cover every surface that she can see. *Just shovel the walk*, she tells herself. *Take down the fake Christmas tree.* It could stay up all year really as it couldn't drop needles if it wanted to. Peter and Lina insisted on it due to 'fire hazard.' Mollie snorts into her tea.

She watches his hands across the table and remembers. Saul centering ten-pound cones of clay on the wheel when she couldn't manage more than four. How they cupped water and set the wheel spinning at high speed. His deft and powerful movements pressing out with the heel of his left hand and pulling in with his right, the clay bumping in rebellion, then quieting to perfect centrifugal calm in a few revolutions. She remembers his hands cracking open belligerent jam jars, wresting rust encrusted plumbing pipes apart with careful control to not strip the threading, splitting kindling with an axe somehow just an extension of his arm. Saul tying fishing flies, exquisite replicas of insects. Saul snipping embedded stitches in the skin of her knee with those same scissors, extracting the suture material so it hadn't hurt her at all.

Saul reaches trembling for the peppershaker. He pushes his plate away, lays the peppershaker on its side and balances his teaspoon across it like a teeter-totter.

"Please eat! We have to be at Dr. Faraday's in an hour." Mollie groans. He looks across the table with the unhearing eyes of a ten-year-old boy. Outside something flickers in the periphery. She glances up just in time to see the owl flash past. He backstrokes, thrusts his legs forward and grasps a branch in the spruce with outstretched furry toes and flaring talons. The wings fold up. The owl performs a vertical hop, his back to the tree trunk. Mastery and movement contained now by silence. He ruffles his feathers and stares. In five minutes when she looks again, she knows the yellow eyes beneath the alert ear tufts will be shut and the bird settled into sleep.

"Look there's one of the owls, I think it's the male." She points, but he's focused on his table top construction, the spoon and the peppershaker exfoliating pepper across the vinyl table cloth. With shaking precision, he places his egg in the bowl of the spoon. "Saul …?" The heel of his right hand descends, a wavering journey ending in exact contact with the lever end. She leaps, very slowly, and her hand stretches hopelessly towards the egg's vacant trajectory. In her prime she'd been a laser quick third baseman. Nothing got past her. She falls back in her chair and the egg catapults across the breakfast nook. It hits a window mullion with a rubbery crack.

"God damn!" Mollie says.

"Did you *see* that? It flew five feet! If I had a bigger spoon …"

"For the love of God, Saul, NO! Sit down. No bigger spoon! And you can damn well eat that egg because I'm not boiling another one!"

"Sorry, Mama!" He grins at her, full of joy from under his weedy white eyebrows.

"*Mollie*, my name is Mollie! Don't call me Mama!" and the hurt confusion on his face fills her with remorse. Then he doubles over with another coughing fit.

"Breathe in again—and again—and again—" Dr. Faraday presses the stethoscope against Saul's back and listens. He takes off the stethoscope and turns to face her.

"How long has he had the cough?"

"Two maybe three weeks, and some fever the last few nights."

"I don't like it. There's definitely congestion in the bottom left lobe. I'm sure he's working on a little pneumonia. I'll write you a prescription. Did you get a pneumonia vaccine this year with your flu shots?" She shakes her head.

"Well after he's better, go get it done. Pneumonia doesn't have to be 'the old man's friend' anymore."

"Oh. Well, was it?"

"I'm sorry, Mollie. Was what?"

"Was it really a 'friend'?"

"I guess. As dying goes it's pretty gentle. They weaken,

just get more and more tired. Some people have anxiety over the loss of breath, but many just slip away quietly in their sleep."

"How long would that take? To die, I mean." Dr. Faraday looks at her. Mollie and Saul have been his patients for fifteen years. He tells his wife about them, Mollie's resolve and loyalty in this dance with a disease, her theory that the Alzheimer's somehow uncovers the different layers of her husband.

"Antibiotics have transformed old age. Before you could lose a senior in three, even two weeks once pneumonia takes hold." Saul hops with his long bony legs off the exam table. He takes the lid off one of the glass jars on the counter, and his hand goes in after the big tongue depressors.

"Can I have a few of these?" he asks, avoiding Mollie's eyes.

"Of course, Saul," Dr. Faraday says.

"Not that many, dear, just take three. Thank you, Bill."

The doctor opens the door of the exam room and Saul hobbles past the nursing station. He stops, drops to his knees and plucks an elastic band from the floor. Mollie rolls her eyes at the doctor but stands back to watch. Now he has his head down almost touching the linoleum, his boney ass in the air as he stretches his arm under a steel trolley and extracts another elastic. Standing, he fits it around the end of one of his tongue depressors, his face lighting up with the projectile possibilities.

Dr. Faraday chuckles. "How long has he been like this? Last year you said he seemed to think he was a high school student again."

Mollie thinks back through the six years since it started, like peeling the layers of an onion, Saul living in reverse. To the friends who shied away from coming to tea she said, in some ways it was a delight, to know all his younger selves.

"I'd swear he's ten now. He's a ten-year-old boy. He's so focused, downright obsessive, endlessly enthusiastic. He doesn't hear anything you tell him if he doesn't want to, and he's always on the go. He must have driven his mother crazy!" They laugh, watching him. Her eyes tear up and she wipes the wet off her gaunt cheekbones.

One morning Saul slips out of the house very early and leaves Mollie sleeping. He puts a bag of cookies in his rucksack, takes his oldest fishing rod and starts walking. He dresses for a summer outing, and luckily this December 23rd registers a mild minus five degrees. Mollie searches the house frantically and can't find him. It isn't until noon when they locate him nine kilometres away, still heading resolutely South on 43rd Street. The city runs on a grid and he envisions the endless street a cutline through the woods, the end surely intersecting the Elbow River of his youth.

She calls her son, Peter. He's at home, thank goodness it being Saturday, and together they drive for miles, phone friends and notify the police. Her teenage grandchildren, Aiden and Moira, and their mum Alice walk the neighbourhood. When there is nothing left to do but wait, the police car finally pulls into Mollie's driveway. Saul sits in the back seat, his tufted white hair alert, his eyes expectant and insatiable, and beside him there's a social worker. A lot of questions follow as to safety in the house and how Mollie manages everything. With assurances that Peter will install keyed deadbolts on both doors, and a referral to an Alzheimer's support group, they finally drive away. But Peter takes the social worker's card, and that night he phones Lina in Toronto.

"Mum, when Peter and Alice get back from Costa Rica in a month, I think I'll fly home. We can meet with this social worker. It's time to take stock of how things are going, how you're coping, you know?"

"What do you mean dear, how I'm coping? Peter installed the deadbolts this afternoon. That's all we need to do. I just have to get him out on walks more, take him to the park and then he doesn't get so restless."

"Mom, you must get so tired! You're seventy-nine! You deserve some rest. You can't be expected to predict everything he's going to do. He's changing all the time. No one person could manage him. Even with dementia Dad's a force of nature. He always has been."

"We manage fine! Peter and the kids help me, and I know him better than anyone. What are you suggesting?"

"At some point, Mum. Well at some point we need to look at other options. Why don't you phone Lucille? She's got her husband in a place. 'Brentwood,' I think? She says it's been a huge relief and that Larry's happy. Why don't you just go have a look, see what you think?"

"Do you remember the Great Horned Owls, Lucille? They're back. I think this is their tenth-year nesting in our yard."

"Oh! The owls! Well, I don't miss them! Hooting all night. Not my favourite birds, and I always worried they'd snatch Bitsy. Harbingers of death, you know. Owls give me the creeps."

"Really? I like them. I thought they symbolized wisdom. Is this it? My, it's very grand!"

Brentview aspires towards a Banff Springs Hotel aesthetic, with a circular drive in front and a clock tower, the unmoving hands arranged artistically at three thirty.

"It's a very luxurious facility. I think Larry feels like a king living here, nothing like our old home. It's the gold standard for dementia care in Calgary from everyone I've talked to. You'll love the staff too; they're just wonderful with him." Then dropping her voice: "He can be so difficult." She holds the door for Mollie, and they go into the vaulted lobby. An immense crystal chandelier hangs down, centered between the embracing arms of a stairwell, descending right and left to a marble floor. Straight ahead of them a fountain burbles. In the middle stands a Grecian maiden looking suspiciously like Farrah Fawcett. She holds an urn that dribbles into the pool around her feet.

"My!" Mollie says.

"Yes, isn't it a beautiful lobby? So stately, I think. Now the dementia wing is this way." And they ascend the red-carpeted stairwell to the right. "It's very secure, I don't have to worry at all about Larry getting lost. I'm sure you'd find it such a relief. Saul couldn't take off on any more of his fishing adventures ..."

Lucille waves an electronic toggle in front of a control panel. A sign on the door reads 'Secure Dementia Wing—Staff and Family Members Only.' The steel doors open soundlessly. They walk through and the doors close behind them with a hermetically sealing hiss and the thud of a locking mechanism falling into place.

"You don't need to worry about windows either. The whole building is air conditioned, so the windows don't need to be operable."

The smell hits her first, disinfectant, shit and piss, and institutional cooking.

"On Wednesdays I think they have Shepherd's Pie and cabbage. The food is really quite good considering. I often come and have lunch with Larry. Family is welcome any time. Oh, they're just finishing up, here they come now."

A shuffling, cataleptic mass of ancient people emerges from the dining room, pushing walkers or being pushed in wheelchairs. Mollie barely recognizes the vacant face of Larry, once so jovial and familiar over the fence. The nursing aide, a young man with myriad piercings and a tattoo of barbed wire around his neck, waves cheerily and pulls the wheelchair to a stop before them.

"Hello, Larry," Mollie says. Larry looks up and doesn't

waste time recognizing who she is, just that she is. He stares into her eyes in a seeming plea and starts pushing alternately with his hands on his armrests rocking his wheelchair from side to side. She can't very well bring up Bitsy the little poodle they kept next door, or how she manages her dandelions now without his input. Maybe make a joke about the hedge going to hell since the new owners? Maybe compliment him on Farrah Fawcett down in the lobby?

"Why don't you stay with him and I'll go get his medication," the body-modified aide says.

"Evenings are hardest," Lucille says. "You'll be feeling better in a minute dear, won't you?"

"What is this? I don't want this!" Larry says, pulling at his seatbelt.

"It's a seatbelt dear. So you don't hurt yourself. Remember you took a few falls."

"But it's boring!" He pins Mollie with his eyes.

"I know, dear. But after your medication you can go watch some hockey in the lounge!" The aide returns. He hands Larry a paper Dixie cup with three pills and another of water. Larry upends them into his mouth, water dribbling down the vertical grooves and random bristles on his chin, the Dixie cup mangled against his face.

"I'll take him now to watch his hockey with the other gents." The aide winks at Mollie, and she realizes with a start that he's had a fake iris tattooed on his lid. The fake iris is blue, and the real iris is brown. The aide grins at her and wheels Larry away.

"We'll say goodbye to him in a minute. Come, I'll

show you his room. It's been such a relief getting him settled. At first it was hard, but now I have so much peace of mind knowing he's safe. You know he was such a good man, a good husband. I couldn't bear it if anything happened to him."

Mollie looks down the hall at the old men arrayed in a circle around the monstrous flat screen TV. One of them sits with his chin resting on his chest. Every thirty seconds he lifts his head and gives off a piercing cry like some jungle bird.

She can't contain herself.

"But don't you see," she says, "don't you see? Something *has* happened to him." But the clatter of a passing trolley drowns out her words.

At Co op Saul keeps acting up, wandering off, or loading the cart with everything he sees. She doesn't have the energy left to fill the prescription at the pharmacy. When they get home, she digs out the kid's old copies of *Tin Tin* and *Asterix and Obelix*. She gives Saul a sandwich, an orange cut into boats, and a glass of milk. He sits cross-legged in the sun reading and laughing while she packs up the Christmas tree. He certainly seems to get the jokes.

"I like Captain Haddock. Listen to this: 'Blistering barnacles! Thundering typhoons! Ectoplasms! Troglodytes! Sea Gherkins! Filibusters!'" Saul rolls over sideways on the rug laughing his scratchy laugh. Then he starts coughing. When he stops, he goes back to *Tin Tin* and reads the same lines all over again, laughing just as hard the second time as the first. "What's a filibuster? I want to swear like Captain Haddock."

"Uh, something to do with politics. Someone who blocks legislation, I think?"

"What's legislation?"

"That's hard to explain. Rules, I guess."

She gets the artificial tree pulled limb from limb and jams it back into its box. Saul sits on it while she tapes it shut.

"That's done. Let's go get the sidewalk shovelled before it's dark. Leave the lights alone now. Come put on your snow pants and a toque and mitts. You can build a fort if you want."

Outside the horizon glows pink below a pale green sky melting into darker and darker blue. The first stars emerge frosty pinpricks in the east. The cold intensifies with the dark, and the snow creaks with every step. Her old ski pants keep her warm, though with her ever shrinking and widening body, she must roll up the cuffs and connect the button to the buttonhole with a looped elastic band.

Saul crawls on all fours pushing snow with his hands and packing it onto his earlier fortifications. Who cares if people saw her retroactively ten-year-old, eighty-year-old husband bellying around in the snow? He could damn well do what he liked. The arthritis in her wrist and shoulder flares with every stroke of the shovel. She shouldn't have waited all day. People pack the snow down with their boots and make it harder. Then she hears the owl, a quiet chuckling chuffing sound, and from the crab-apple beside the garage, an answering hoot.

"Listen, Saul. Listen! The owls are back for sure. They've started their calling." Softly now, distant, mournful, the male answers the female: "Who-who-who—Who-who." He's roosted in the tree right above them. Saul sits bolt upright in the snow.

"They're an old mated pair. In January they call to each other through the night. It's a bonding ritual. By February they'll stop. I always miss it when you can't hear them anymore. You used to tell me they laid their eggs then, in February. They're the earliest nesting birds in Canada."

Now with full amplitude approaching the passion of a train whistle, the male calls again. "WHO-WHO—Who-who-who." Saul cranes his head to see. He pulls his mittens off and cups his hands together, then blows into the crack between his thumbs to make a loon call in the tradition of children. At first, he only produces a dry whuffling, but then some muscle memory kicks in and he gets it. "Who-who-who," and the female answers from the back yard. So, he'd known how to do that since he was ten. Saul capers about the snow in a frenzy.

"They're talking to me!"

"Shhhh, don't shout. You'll scare them. Try it again, call them." She finishes shovelling, listening to Saul talking to the owls and remembering him calling them for the grandchildren on the back porch.

They finish eating stew and toast. The infection isn't slowing him down yet. As usual he tries the kitchen door after dinner, twists and pulls on the knob and stares in perplexity at the deadbolt.

"I'm going out. I want to check my rabbit trap. Why doesn't this open? Where is the key?"

"Your rabbit trap?"

"Yes, by the barn." Don't argue, she tells herself. Distract.

"Remember the owls?" Saul stops and looks at her.

"With the big nest?"

"Yes! Come watch this movie. It's all about owls." And she manages to park him in front of a BBC bird documentary.

The phone rings. It is Peter.

"Hi Mom. How are you doing? How's dad?"

"We're fine, dear."

"Well, we're leaving in two days for Costa Rica. Is there anything you need done before we go? Want us to come over and watch dad for a while? You could go out and get a break, have lunch or get a haircut or something."

"That would be good. Thank you. Bring the kids if they're free. Saul loves to see them." Mollie tries to organize the papers on the counter with the phone squeezed between her ear and shoulder. She needs to read through them but is tempted to just sweep them into the garbage.

"By the way, you never told me how you liked Lucille's nursing home. What did you think of it?"

"Hmm, what's that dear?"

"What did you think of Brentwood Manor, where Lucille put Larry?"

"Oh! You mean, Brentview? Well. I thought it was God-awful actually. A tarted-up prison, that's what I thought of it." Peter laughs at the other end of the line.

"Well, that's only one facility. We can look around."

"He has advanced Alzheimer's, Peter! He's a very determined wanderer. One lock down dementia ward is the same as any other. Besides Lucille says Brentwood is the 'gold standard for dementia care in Calgary.'"

"Well, we can look around." He repeats himself. "You have a month anyhow to think about things before we get back, and then Lina will come and we'll sort out what's best."

What's best? What's best, she thinks. I'll tell you what's best. Peter managing her, the way one would manage a child, offering her her options. Rather than shout, she just hangs up the phone.

Saul stands at the back door in his slippers. He pulls on the handle and peers at the lock.

"I need to check my rabbit trap."

After his bath Saul sits in his twin bed, the lamp illuminating silver eyebrows and tufty hair. Two years ago, when he decided he was a teenager and that Mollie was his mother, he refused to sleep in their double bed anymore. She told herself his midnight wanderings disturbed her sleep anyhow and turned the small study beside the kitchen into a boy's bedroom.

"Tonight, I'm going to read you a new book. It's

about a wizard and a boy, and I know you'll find it interesting because the wizard has an owl called Archimedes. Archimedes can talk!"

"He can talk like a person?"

"Yes, I suppose he's magic. The magician has a trick to him too. He knows everything that is going to happen to the boy already. He has come to teach the boy, so he will grow up to be the next king."

"How does he know already?"

"Well, I don't quite understand, but while the boy lives his life forwards, the wizard lives his life backwards, so he's already done everything with the boy before and he knows what will happen next."

"I think I see."

"In each chapter the wizard turns the boy into a different sort of animal, so he can learn what it's like. Should I begin? It's called *The Sword in the Stone*."

She skimmed through the first bit which dragged and was too complex, she thinks, for Saul to grasp, till she gets to the good part: "*'We see so little company,' explained the magician, wiping his head with half a worn-out pair of pyjamas, which he kept for that purpose, 'that Archimedes is a little shy of strangers. Come, Archimedes, I want you to meet a friend of mine called Wart.'*" And Mollie reads how Merlin taught the boy to get the owl on his finger. Saul lies back against the pillow his eyes half closed. So rarely still. The words and the rhythm soothe him and his memory for narrative seems somehow more entrenched. It is a blessing. He can still watch movies and enjoy a bedtime story. Mollie stops at the end of the chapter where Merlin tells

Wart, to his delight, that he will come back to Sir Hector's castle as his permanent tutor.

"There," Mollie says, closing the book. "Roll over for your backrub. You're heating up again. I'll get you some Advil and then you'll sleep." When she returns from the kitchen, he is lying on his back staring at the ceiling, his papery cheeks too pink. "Sit up. There you go. Swallow these." When he lies flat, he starts to cough so she props him up with more pillows.

In the kitchen she put on her boots and takes the compost bucket off the counter. She walks out the back door and down the steps, through the snow to the compost bin Saul built so long ago. "You'll just bring in the mice with that," she hears Lucille comment over the fence. Mollie lifts the heavy wood and chicken wire lid, and indeed mice scurry as she throws in the banana peels and coffee grounds. *Well, I have to feed my owls*, she thinks.

As Mollie returns to the back porch, one hoots in the old spruce, and she hears Saul answer from inside his room. She goes into the kitchen and takes off her boots. While washing out the stinking bucket, she sees Dr. Faraday's prescription in a jumble of mail. She dries her hands, picks it up and sticks it to the fridge with a magnet. She stands looking at it. Four weeks, she thinks. I have four weeks.

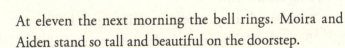

At eleven the next morning the bell rings. Moira and Aiden stand so tall and beautiful on the doorstep.

"Grandma!" They embrace her.

"Dad's running around like crazy, so he just dropped us off," Moira says. Mollie peers down the street and waves to the vanishing SUV.

"Come in! How are you doing? Grandpa will be so happy to see you! Saul, the kids are here!" Saul emerges from the gloom of the hallway all his yellow teeth exposed in a huge grin, the white hair standing on end.

"Hello, Saul," Aiden says. "How about a game of checkers?" In an undertone to Mollie: "He couldn't do crib last time, but he's still pretty good at checkers."

"Hello, Rob. Hello, Margey! Can they stay all afternoon?"

Moira winks at Mollie and Aiden goes with Saul to find the checkerboard.

"My beautiful granddaughter," Mollie says, reaching up with both hands to smooth Moira's hair back and tuck it behind her ears. "You must be so excited! You have to take lots of pictures for me."

"I will, but I'm going to miss you, Grandma. Do you want me to do a once over in Saul's room? Make sure he's not been up to his old tricks again?"

"Oh yes, I forget to do that. That would be a great help. I think he's moved beyond his camping phase, but you never know."

"Remember when he turned sixteen again? How he kept flirting with teenage girls at the grocery story? Girls with long brown hair."

"Oh dear, that was hard to explain, wasn't it?"

"But you didn't get mad. Didn't it hurt your feelings?"

"Well, I had long brown hair when he met me, so I

took it as a kind of compliment." Mollie stops. "I'd better go darling and do my shopping. It won't be so easy once everyone's away."

Instead of driving over the Eighty-Fifth Street Bridge to Co op, Mollie turns left and then right into the park. The air is crystalline in the cold sunshine and the park very quiet this winter afternoon. She gets out of the car and follows a path west through the gloom of the Douglas Fir Trail. At the end she reaches a bay notched into the tail of the island. There, a metre or so out from the bank, sits a mountain of a rock surrounded by ice. Saul had thought it a glacial erratic. No matter how high or violent the spring floods, it remained immoveable year after year. She scuffs over the ice, half walking half sliding so she won't fall. The east side is easier to climb, a lower slope with some notched out cracks for finger and footholds. She manages to scramble to the top without dropping her purse and sits facing out towards the open water beyond the ice. The sun warms her back through her coat even as her face stings with the cold. She can see Saul out ahead of her in his waders, the long line of his fly rod whipping out and around him, catching the sunlight and flinging drops of water. She sits there till the sun begins to set, and then very stiff and cold she returns to the car and drives to Co op.

In Co op Mollie stops and doesn't know what to do. The cart overflows with colour, citrus fruit, broccoli, a roast, food to sustain life. How do you feed someone so that they can die? She retraces her steps and puts a bunch of it away. She buys four bottles each of Ibuprofen and Tylenol, and bag of chicken backs to make soup. He'll have to eat something, at least for the first while. She gets microwaveable dinners for herself. Perishables could be ordered on the computer since Co op delivers. For now, she buys milk, eggs, cheese and a little fruit for the coming week.

Next Mollie stops at the library and takes out the limit of twenty CDs, picking subjects Saul will like: nature documentaries, a boxed set of a fishing and hunting series, the history of King Arthur. Under the circumstances she has no idea what to read herself. After the library she drives to the bank, takes out a lot of cash, and pays the bills.

Peter stands in the kitchen. The kids and Saul laugh in the living room.

"Are you all organized for the trip dear?" Peter doesn't answer.

"Mum, what's this?" He holds out Dr. Faraday's prescription. "It's dated five days ago. This should have been filled right away." His forehead furrows and his eyes verge on frantic. "Why haven't you done this? Dad's got quite a cough!"

Mollie looks down at her boots. "Oh dear," she says lamely. "That keeps slipping my mind. We'll go and do it first thing tomorrow morning."

"Hi Grandma." Moira comes into the room.

"And what's this that Moira's been telling me? She found matches and newspaper and twigs in little bundles under Dad's bed today. She says she's found similar bundles *four* times before. Why didn't you tell me this?"

Moira looks back and forth between her grandma and father, her eyes big and her lips pressed together.

Mollie laughs lightly. "Oh, Saul must still be in his camping phase, but I've gotten rid of all the matches now, I can't imagine when he got that last set, so now that Moira's found them everything is fine. You'd better get going, hadn't you? I'm sure there's still lots to pack and you have to leave so early." Moira comes up close beside her.

"I'm sorry, Grandma," she says in a low voice.

"There's nothing to be sorry about, darling. Don't worry. Everything will be fine." Then louder: "Saul, come and say goodbye to Peter and the kids."

Peter runs his hands through his hair, a sheen of sweat on his forehead. "Well, I don't have time to deal with this, I guess." His eyes scan the cluttered disorganized kitchen and come at last to rest on Mollie. "Well. Keep safe."

When they leave Mollie closes the door and turns the key in the deadbolt. She stands for a moment with her eyes shut, her back against the cold door, and then goes and puts the key in its hiding place.

That evening she makes a huge pot of chicken soup. The compost bucket overflows with the onion skins and celery ends, carrot peelings, the squeezed-out lemons. After its simmered for an hour, she carries the stew pot to the sink and dumps everything, the chicken bones, the vegetables and broth, into a colander lined with cheesecloth on top of her canning kettle. Then she chops up more fresh vegetables and adds them to the pot with some white rice, dried thyme, salt and pepper. She sets it to boil again. The clock reads six fifty. No time for anything but bacon and eggs for dinner. The soup she'll freeze in her vast supply of empty cottage cheese containers.

At eight Saul splashes around in the bathroom brushing his teeth. The phone rings.

"Hi, Mum," Lina says.

"Hello, dear."

"Mum, I had a talk with Peter last night. I don't know what to say. I'm afraid you're not going to be happy with this, with Peter and me. It's just that, it's just that he and I are both really worried, and now he's going to be gone for a month ..."

"What are you worried about, dear? What do you mean?"

"He said Dad has been hiding matches? He said he's really sick, but you haven't filled a subscription he needs. He said the house seems out of control ... The long and short of it is we've decided that we can't wait till Peter gets back to meet with the social worker. I'm going to come to Calgary right away. I've booked a ticket for Wednesday."

"But that's tomorrow. It's Tuesday today."

"Mum, how to say this?" She decides just to talk very quickly. "I think it's time I became Dad's legal guardian.

You're just too emotionally involved to make the sort of decisions that have to be made."

"*What?*"

"He could set a fire or something. You could burn in your beds. Peter and I, we couldn't live with ourselves if something like that happened. You do understand, Mum? We just couldn't bear to lose you guys."

Mollie doesn't remember what else they say to each other. When she hangs up the phone, her hand shakes so she can hardly nest the receiver in the cradle. Saul calls from his bedroom.

"Are we going to read? It's time for stories!"

Mollie stumbles into the living room and moves the books and papers piled up on the fold down lid of the liquor cabinet. She roots around behind and pulls out a bottle, Crown Royal. Anything will do. She brings it into the kitchen and pours two fingers into a glass and drinks it very fast. The alcohol burns her mouth and inside her nose and scorches her throat all the way down to her entrails. She stands holding onto the counter as the heat radiates through her. She breathes and the shaking stops.

"I'm going to read you the chapter where the magician turns the boy into a hawk. It's been raining a lot and Wart is very bored and he begs Merlin to turn him into another animal. Merlin decides that this time he should be a bird." Mollie starts and miraculously, as always happens, she gets lost in the reading.

"Roll over," she says and slides her hands up under his pyjama top. She works slowly down his wrinkly neck, his spine. His back is still surprisingly muscular. He sighs deeply and nestles further into the pillow. She rakes her fingers gently over and over through his silver hair.

"Do you know what I'm going to do tomorrow, Ma?"

"No, what?"

"I'm going to tame that owl, so he'll sit on my shoulder."

"Good night, darling," she says and kisses his cheek for a long time, breathing in the particular musk of his skin. He radiates heat from the incubating infection. She goes and gets him two Advil.

"Listen for the owls. They'll be starting up soon."

In the kitchen the compost bucket overflows with the vegetable peelings from the soup. She puts on her boots and coat and gets the key from its hiding place on the cookbook shelf.

Outside the snow squawks and crackles as Mollie walks. Stars riddle the sky and she floats because of the whiskey. After emptying the bucket into the compost bin, she goes back inside. Saul coughs in his bed. He hears her and rolls over, watching in the light from the kitchen as she hangs her coat on the back of a chair. She pours herself another dose of whiskey and does her best to shoot it, choking in the attempt but getting most of it down.

"Is that medicine?"

"Yes. I don't feel well." Mollie takes the key out of the deadbolt. She holds it up, so he can see and then reinserts it into the lock. She doesn't even turn it, making it as easy as possible. Neither does she switch off the kitchen light. Clumping in her snow boots she starts to leave the kitchen.

"Goodnight, Ma."

"Goodnight, darling."

Don't look up. Just go. She watches her feet, left right, left right. In the living room she crawls into the embrace of his old leather recliner. Sitting down, the bottle in one hand, the glass in the other, she pours herself another drink, this time three fingers, and swallows it in two gulps. She puts the Crown Royal on the floor and, reaching with her right hand, hauls on the wooden lever. The chair unfolds with a two-point lurch that throws her onto her back. Mollie lies there and watches the silver sparkles on the blown plaster ceiling. The last thing she hears is Saul talking to the owls.

In the morning she wakes with a seismic headache and a mouth full of sand. Never has she felt so thirsty and so, so, cold. *I am sick with some God-awful flu*, she thinks. *Maybe I've caught Saul's pneumonia and I'm about to start a fever and that's why I'm so cold?* She realizes only her feet are warm because she's still wearing winter boots. Her eyes fly open to gape at the living room ceiling.

"Oh my God, *Saul!*" She starts shouting even as she struggles out of the recliner. Her leg gets caught in the metal hinge of the footrest. She wrenches it free and falls. From all fours on the living room carpet, Mollie stares down the hallway into the kitchen. The back door swings a little in the wind, silence except for the soft brushing of blown snow across the linoleum. "*SAUL*," she screams again, and half-staggers half-runs into the kitchen where she vomits into the sink. While she's retching, she prays:

I will look up and he'll be sleeping in his little bed, his back turned to me under the rocket ship duvet. He will roll over, his hair all standing on end in the morning sun and ask if I'm sick.

The vomiting ends. She looks up and his bed lies empty, the duvet thrown off with purpose and abandon. "Oh no, oh my beloved. Oh no."

I will go outside, she thinks. *I will go outside, and he'll have made a fire out of all the fire bundles piled behind the garbage can. He'll smile and say he wants to cook breakfast on his campfire, and I will bring him bacon and a frying pan …*

Mollie walks to the back door and stands looking at the snow blowing hard and sideways over the compacted drifts. The wind chill cuts her face in seconds, but she doesn't think of a coat. She crosses the back deck and stands at the top of the stairs. Footsteps, half eroded by the wind, make a straight line for the owl tree. The old male sits in his customary spot against the trunk out of the wind, absorbing any heat he can from the sun. Her boot measures three inches shorter than the footstep in the snow and she follows them carefully, placing her foot in each one. As she comes within three metres of the tree, the owl shifts on his white pantalooned legs, black talons flaring and gripping in anxiety.

"Where is Saul?!" she demands of him. The owl rises up, bobbing in accordion feathered alarm. *"Where is he?"* Mollie screams and the bird hunkers down. He stretches forward and leaps. The wings unfold, and the downbeat of the take-off blows her hair back in the total silence of an owl in flight. Four wing beats and he's cleared the yard. She inhales the hard air, welcoming the advancing anaesthesia of the cold, and steps under the branches, into the cathedral of the old spruce. Saul's well-worn slippers lie there in the needles and dirt. *I won't look up*, she thinks. *I just won't look up.* Ice crystals dance in diagonal shafts of sunlight, splitting into motes of red or green, silver or gold.

"Mollie."

"Yes, Saul!"

"Hold your hands up."

"Saul?"

"Just for a moment. The parents are hunting. I'll hand you down a chick and then I'll put him right back."

"Won't the parents abandon them if they smell us?" She hears her own voice and raises her hands and eyes above her head. Saul smiles down at her, dark hair, dark eyes, the specks of light slowly swirling in front of him.

"No, I don't think so. They're too invested. Here, just hold him for a moment."

Her hands reach and stretch, and she sees the hoar frosted fuzz of the chick, feels the warm beating lightness of him, the thin skin beneath the feathers. The ebony beak and black-circled eyes pin her with their stare. And then the yellow irises and black pupils blink, just once. Her hands stretch empty of the fuzz and the warmth, and slumped over a branch, curled towards the trunk, nests her silent and unmoving Saul.

Acknowledgements

This collection largely took shape in English 496 *Short Fiction*, at the University of Calgary. Thank you to my fellow classmates for their insightful critiques and camaraderie, and to Aritha van Herk for her exceptional teaching and mentorship.

For helping me find the courage to start, thank you to the Alexandra Writer's Centre.

To the friends and family who read, supported, and offered feedback, thank you. You know who you are.

Lori Hahnel guided and educated me when it came time to publish, a munificent and unexpected gift.

Thank you to Michael Mirolla of Guernica Editions, for his expert editing and making publication such a seamless and enjoyable experience. Thank you to David Moratto for really getting a feel for my book, and the resulting beautiful cover design.

To my three children Avery, Nathan, and Josephine, thank you for your forbearance with your distracted mother, and your kind interest and enthusiasm. A special thank you to Avery, for getting his brother and sister to bed when I was at class and their dad was working late. Finally, to Paul, for keeping us so safe, my love always.

About the Author

Sophie Stocking writes, illustrates, and parents in Calgary Alberta. Her first novel *Corridor Nine,* was published by Thistledown Press in 2019.

About the Author

Noelle Bicking works as illustrator and printmaker in Calgary, Alberta. Her first novel *Cold as Wine* was published by Thunderwood Press in 2019.

This book is made of paper from well-managed FSC® - certified forests, recycled materials, and other controlled sources.

 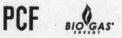